A KILLER'S TARGET

DANA R. LYNN

Recycling programs for this product may not exist in your area.

ISBN-13: 978-1-335-91905-2

A Killer's Target

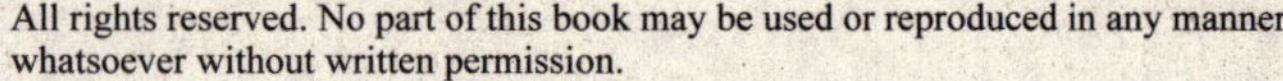

For questions and comments about the quality of this book, please contact us at CustomerService@Harlequin.com.

® is a trademark of Harlequin Enterprises ULC.

Love Inspired
22 Adelaide St. West, 41st Floor
Toronto, Ontario M5H 4E3, Canada
www.LoveInspired.com

HarperCollins Publishers
Macken House, 39/40 Mayor Street Upper,
Dublin 1, D01 C9W8, Ireland
www.HarperCollins.com

Printed in Lithuania

1 2 3 4 5 6 7 8 9 10 LIT 28 27 26 25

"He's set both porches on fire," Brett exclaimed.

"We're trapped?"

"No. We're not trapped. We'll go out through the attic. There's a trapdoor. Then a tree. Follow me."

She didn't have much choice. Already the smoke was filtering into the house.

He placed his hands on a large panel on the ceiling and shoved it sideways. It slid away, creating an entrance.

Brett helped her into the attic, then slammed the panel shut again. There was a small window at one end of the attic.

About six inches away from the window, a thick branch extended to a large tree. Another branch on the other side ended near the roof of the barn.

"You want me to climb not one but two branches?"

"It's the only way out."

The smoke smell had thickened. The temperature in the room had risen at least ten degrees since they had entered the room.

"Go," he told her. "I'll be right behind you."

Leila hefted herself onto the window ledge and inched her way out and onto the tree limb, praying that she and Brett would both come out the other end of this adventure alive...

Dana R. Lynn grew up in Illinois. She met her husband at a wedding and told her parents she'd met the man she was going to marry. Nineteen months later, they were married. Today, they live in rural Pennsylvania with their three children and a variety of animals. In addition to writing, she works as a teacher for the deaf and hard of hearing, and is active in her church.

Books by Dana R. Lynn

Love Inspired Suspense

Amish Country Danger

Amish Midwife Witness
A Killer's Target

Amish Country Justice

Hidden in Amish Country
Plain Refuge
Deadly Amish Reunion
Amish Country Threats
Covert Amish Investigation
Amish Christmas Escape
Amish Cradle Conspiracy
Her Secret Amish Past
Crime Scene Witness
Hidden Amish Target
Hunted at Christmas
Amish Witness to Murder
Protecting the Amish Child
Hunting the Amish Witness

Visit the Author Profile page at LoveInspired.com for more titles.

For God hath not given us the spirit of fear;
but of power, and of love, and of a sound mind.

—*2 Timothy* 1:7

To my graduate, Gregory. I am so proud of you and blessed to be your mom.

ONE

"Wait! Don't touch that!" Forensic photographer Leila Britton grabbed her camera bag and slammed the door of her SUV, never taking her eyes from the teenage boys standing close—way too close—to the body lying curled on the raised bank of French Creek.

"We weren't going to touch her," the taller boy replied, hunching his shoulders, his jaw jutted. The younger boy kept his gaze on the ground and his hands fisted in his pockets. She hadn't meant to scare them.

"Look, I know you meant no harm." She smiled at them. It probably looked fake. "I'm the forensic photographer. I need to get this scene photographed before anything gets moved. So we can catch whoever did this."

There was no doubt in her mind this was a murder scene. The woman's hands were duct-taped together. So were her ankles. A quick glance showed a third band around her knees. The creep responsible for this hadn't wanted to take any chances she'd escape her fate. "Are you the ones who found her and called 911?"

They shook their heads.

"No, ma'am." The taller boy, obviously the spokesperson, pointed to the kayak in the bed of a pickup truck.

"We'd been kayaking but decided to pack it in when we saw the sky."

"Did you happen to see anyone else in the area?"

Both boys shook their heads.

If they didn't call 911, who did? According to the request for a forensic photographer, the dispatcher had said the caller hung up after reporting the body. She hadn't said the caller sounded like a kid, though. A chill worked its way down her spine. The spot between her shoulder blades prickled.

Was someone watching her? She turned in a full circle, her gaze scanning the surrounding area. When nothing menacing popped out at her, she returned to her original position. The air had a slight bite to it.

She glanced at the sky. Dark clouds gathered on the horizon. Even the air smelled like a storm was coming. They needed the rain. The summer had been unusually dry for this part of rural northwestern Pennsylvania. But for it to storm today of all days! She needed to work quickly to preserve the scene.

"Did you pull her from the water?" She returned her gaze to the boys.

Their eyes widened. "No, ma'am! She was here when we saw her."

Leila nodded and glanced around. Where were the police? "Stay close. I'm sure the police will want to talk to you."

A single police car pulled up to the curb. A young female officer wearing a gray uniform with sleek golden-blond hair pinned up in a bun emerged. Leila hadn't met her yet. Which wasn't unusual. Although she worked in conjunction with the departments in the region, Leila was employed by an outside forensics lab that contracted with various police stations.

Leila rushed over to her. The sooner they were introduced, the sooner she could begin on the crime scene. She glanced at the woman's badge. Officer Michaela Witt.

"Officer Witt. Hi. I'm Leila Britton, the forensic photographer." She tried to smile, but it felt awkward. She'd always been an introvert but was determined to force herself to be social. At least at work.

The young officer nodded a greeting, her lips parting in a friendly smile. "I apologize if you've been here long."

"Not that long." Leila pointed to the logo on the side of the cruiser. "I understand why it took a while. This is quite a distance from the Sterling Ridge Police Department." At least a twenty-five-minute drive. "Are others coming?"

Small departments didn't always have the manpower they needed. Leila had been asked just yesterday to take on the department in her rotation. The photographer who normally worked with Sterling Ridge had quit suddenly. Leila wasn't happy about adding another department to her rotation. She had nothing against Sterling Ridge. Distance-wise, it was convenient for her since she'd lived there for the past two years. She already worked for several departments, though. It would stretch her, but she needed the paycheck. She was a young widow with a four-year-old to raise. It had taken nearly two years to get her life back together after Will had died three and a half years ago. Evie had been just a baby. That didn't mean she accepted what had happened. Every time she recalled her shame when he'd died from carbon monoxide poisoning in his mistress's company, anger burned inside. Both bodies had been recovered, sleeping in the same bed. Once she'd realized she'd need to return to work to support herself and her daughter, she'd started searching and quickly learned she had limited opportunities that used her skills and education that paid well enough for them to survivé independently. For the past three years, she'd made her place as a forensic photographer. Maybe in a few years, when Evelyn was older, she'd rethink her career options.

Officer Witt responded to her question, dragging Leila's mind back to the present.

"Yes, ma'am. Lieutenant Talbot has a team on the way. I just happened to be close to the area."

Good. She'd never met this Lieutenant Talbot, but she couldn't wait. Every second wasted meant the scene could be contaminated.

"Thanks. Do me a favor? I need you to stay back and make sure nothing and no one bothers the crime scene until the others arrive. I need to start working before the storm comes in." Already, she felt the breeze picking up.

"Sure, I can do that."

As she turned her gaze back to the scene, only her years of professional experience kept her from wincing.

She had been to multiple murder scenes since she'd entered the field. But nothing had prepared her for the sight when she'd first arrived. Weeds tangled with the victim's shoulder-length dark hair. In addition to her hands and feet, duct tape also sealed the victim's mouth. The horror hadn't lessened while she'd talked with Officer Witt.

It had been a long time since she'd seen a crime scene that hit her this hard. The worst one happened nearly ten years previous. But at that time, the scene had been far more personal. She slammed the door on the memories threatening to shake her calm.

"Was she pulled from the water?" Leila turned away and

faced Officer Witt. And away from the water. She was too close to it. The acid roiled in her stomach. She wouldn't let her fear of water control her. She took a couple of slow, deep breaths. She needed to regain her composure. "The two boys over there said she was out of the water when they arrived on scene."

"I don't think so. The caller just said there was a body near the water."

She tightened her muscles to hold off a shudder. To her overactive imagination, it sounded like the person who'd called in was being cryptic. She shoved the thought away. She'd explore that avenue later.

She shifted her camera bag to keep the strap from sliding off her shoulder. Her boots slipped on the muddy bank. She caught herself before she disgraced herself and fell like a rookie, then checked the zipper to ensure her Nikon D850 was secure. It was her favorite camera, one she'd saved money for months to buy.

She exhaled slowly, forcing herself to focus. She knew her photographs would preserve the evidence so the officers could process the scene and begin searching for the monster who did this.

She stepped past the boys and drew closer to the deceased woman lying on the muddy ground, curled up as if she were asleep. She slowly walked around the scene, being careful not to disturb anything.

Leila lifted her camera and began snapping pictures, quickly falling into the meticulous pattern.

She started with wide-angle shots of the entire scene. She spent several minutes capturing the entire landscape, including the officer present. She snapped the body where it lay, making sure to get enough of the background. The investigators would need to know the body's position. She took out her ruler and measured the distance between the body and the nearest tree and from the water, documenting it in the small notebook she kept in her camera bag.

Now for the difficult part. She moved in for shots of the body and immediate area, paying close attention to the duct tape around the woman's wrists, knees and ankles. Judging from her sweatpants, cotton T-shirt and top-of-the-line running shoes, she'd been a jogger. It was possible she'd been snatched while on her morning run.

Just like Tara had been.

Leila wrenched her mind away from her twin sister. She had a job to do and couldn't afford to be distracted from doing it.

Tara's killer had never been found. She would do her best to make sure this woman's family didn't suffer the same as she and her parents had. Her family hadn't had the opportunity to fully work through the grieving process. The lack of closure was an open wound that ate away at a person. It had nearly destroyed her parents' marriage. In the end, they had sold the house and moved to Colorado, almost as far away from here as they could get. Her father stayed there when her mother passed away.

She'd get as much from this scene as she could to spare this woman's family the same pain.

Lifting her camera again, she did a close-up of the victim's face, noting the blue lips. When she moved on to the victim's body, she noted the vascular marbling, the dark discolorations marking her skin, indicating she'd been submerged in water. Had she been held down and drowned? The watch strapped to her wrist glowed slightly. No. She couldn't have been underwater for long. But how did she get to be here? The water wasn't high enough for a body to wash up on the bank. And there were no drag marks. Or footprints.

She was missing something. Conviction settled on her. This wasn't the full crime scene.

"Miss Britton?"

She turned to Officer Witt. "Call me Leila."

"Leila, then. I just got a text from the lieutenant. He and his team are five minutes out."

"Good. I don't think this is the whole crime scene. I'm going to see if there's anything beyond those trees. Let me know when the team arrives, please. I would like to share a few of my impressions with them."

"I will. What do you want me to do in the meantime?"

Leila blinked. She wasn't used to being in charge. "Interview those two." She waved a finger to one boy, then the other. "And make sure nothing disturbs the scene."

She'd already said that, but she'd seen too many crime scenes contaminated by careless mistakes in the past.

Leila exchanged camera lenses and made her way to the trees, walking as if glass littered the ground. She didn't want to step on any evidence. And she knew there was more out there.

She stepped behind the trees and blinked. Without the open sky, dappled shadows fell over everything. She reached back for the flashlight in her bag.

A strong arm wrapped around her stomach, and a hand covered her mouth, the grip so tight, she couldn't even open her mouth to bite. She tried to knock her head back against her attacker's nose, but she was too short. If she could hook a leg around his, maybe she could trip him. She strained against him, but the man holding her lifted her until her toes barely scrapped the dirt.

The aroma of tobacco overwhelmed her. Her lungs tightened. She fought, squirming in his arms, but he began to drag her away from the scene, inch by inch.

One thought flooded her mind: She'd never see her baby again.

Lieutenant Brett Talbot arrived on scene. Immediately behind him, three other police cruisers pulled along the curb. Soon eight officers were on the scene.

"Officer Witt," he called to the young woman.

She held up a finger, said a few words to the two teenagers with her, then released them. She jogged in his direction. "Sir?"

"I thought you said the forensic photographer was on scene." He scanned the area. No one unfamiliar popped into view. "I can't remember what Chief Kaiser said her name was."

"Leila Britton, sir. She's already photographed the scene. She went to investigate behind the trees. That was only about five minutes ago."

He narrowed his eyes at the sky. The clouds swirled above them, eating up the blue sky that had been there only an hour earlier. "I'm going to go find her. We need to work fast. That storm is only minutes away."

"I'll start directing everything here, Brett." Lieutenant Carter Flint, Brett's best friend since they were children, walked past him and clapped a hand on his shoulder.

"Appreciate that, Carter." With Carter taking over for him, he had no worries about not being front and center for a few minutes.

He approached the thick cluster of trees along the walkway. It was dim, so he pulled out his phone and used the flashlight app. The first thing he saw was a camera bag lying on its side, contents spilling haphazardly on the damp ground. An expensive-looking camera rested on a patch of moss a few feet away.

No forensic photographer would treat such pricey tools of their trade so casually.

He darted back out of the trees. Sergeant Brian Roberts and Lieutenant Ryan Douglass were standing nearby. He called out to them, "Something happened to the forensic photographer."

The two men exchanged worried glances and joined him immediately. A third officer loped over.

Brian peered at the area. Then he suddenly pointed to the ground. "There! Looks like she was dragged."

"And she was struggling," Ryan said, pointing to the scuff marks in the dirt.

Before Brett could respond, he heard a woman shriek in the distance, pain and rage melded in the sharp sound.

Brett knew that sound. He'd protected his mother from his abusive father for far too many years. By the time he'd turned eighteen, he'd already learned more about the deceitful facades people wear than most people learn in a lifetime.

It was the reason he became a Marine and later a cop, bringing his best friend along with him for both. He wouldn't let the photographer come to harm if he could help it. He had to get to her in time.

Leaping over a fallen tree stump, he hurtled through the foliage and across the grass toward another copse of pine trees. He heard the footsteps of his colleagues tromping behind him. They would find this woman and bring her to safety.

And hopefully a criminal to justice.

A man shouted.

Brett pounded through an opening in the trees in time to see a man in a Grim Reaper mask, running shorts and a T-shirt shake off a woman who had his arm clamped tightly in her teeth. They were standing beside the main road leading to Saegertown.

The assailant raised a hand to slap her.

"Police!" Brett raised his Glock and aimed at the man. "Let her go!"

The assailant tossed the young woman toward the street, into the path of an oncoming truck. She stumbled and cried out, her leg crumpling beneath her. Brett charged across the first lane and swooped her up. They landed in a tangle on the side of the road as the truck driver honked his horn and sailed by. The curls around the photographer's head blew across her face from the draft of the vehicle's passing.

The moment the road was clear, Brian and Officer Joe Maillard raced off in pursuit of the assailant.

Brett looked down at the photographer. "Leila?"

"Yeah." She groaned and sat up. "Thank you for saving me. I was sure I was going to die."

Brett rose to his feet. He scoured the area before turning his gaze back to her. "Are you hurt badly?"

"I don't think so." She wiped her sleeve across her bloody mouth. When his gaze zeroed in, she flushed. "It's his blood. Not mine. Ugh. I need mouthwash."

The strange comment made him laugh.

Realizing she was still on the ground, he held out his hand and helped her stand. As she placed all her weight on her feet, she winced.

"Did you injure your ankle?"

She shook her head. "It's probably sprained. But I can walk."

Ryan approached. "I got your bag."

"My cameras!" She snatched the bag from him with a hasty thanks. When she peered inside, some of the tension drained from her posture. "My Nikon is here. I dropped it when he grabbed me. I have all the crime scene pictures on it."

Brett gestured in the direction they had come from. The group strode back. After the first few steps, Brett nodded, satisfied her ankle wasn't hampering her ability to keep up with them. "Why did you leave the scene?"

"Well..." She paused as her eyes dropped to his name tag. "Lieutenant Talbot, I finished the crime scene pictures."

He nodded. "That's what Michaela said. And it's Brett."

"Pleasure to meet you." They arrived back at the original scene. She pointed to the body. "But I realized there was no way this was the actual crime scene."

He pursed his lips, nodding. "Go on."

He hadn't had time to study the scene yet, but he'd already noticed a few inconsistencies.

"Her clothes are soaked and her skin is mottled. I suspect she was in the water, but not too long. The watch on her wrist was still working. If she'd been under for more than a few hours, her watch, even if it were waterproof, wouldn't still be working. And the water is low enough that there is no way she could have washed up on shore. And there are no drag marks on the ground."

"She'd been placed there purposely."

"That's my belief."

Brett narrowed his eyes and viewed the body. It made sense. "The caller didn't say he'd *found* a body. He said there *is* a body."

"You think the caller is the one who put the body here." Her tone said she'd come to the same conclusion.

"I do."

A fat raindrop smacked his forehead. Followed quickly

by a second. Beside him, Leila shivered, no doubt realizing she'd nearly been another victim. Which was too close to be a coincidence.

"Officer Witt."

The young officer strode over to them. "Sir?"

"Just a moment." He turned back to Leila.

"Leila, I'm going to have you wait in my cruiser. Officer Witt will accompany you." She started to protest, and he raised a hand to silence her. "You're shivering. I don't want you to go into shock. At the moment, you are more than our forensic photographer. You are the closest thing to a witness we have."

"Witness?"

"We both know the man who tried to abduct you was probably the murderer. No one wears any kind of costume mask in July. I think you got too close to him. He couldn't have you identify him."

"But I never saw him."

"No. But that wouldn't have stopped him from making you his second victim."

Leila's brown eyes widened. Her face grew so pale he feared she'd pass out. He stretched out a hand to steady her. She shook her head and gave him a tight smile. "I'm good. Really."

His hand dropped back to his side. While he watched, the color returned to her cheeks, though the shadows never left her eyes.

Brett wasn't one who thrived on adrenaline. He liked his world orderly. He always showed up to meetings early and never left until they were finished. His reports were on time every time. Procrastination wasn't in his makeup. And he disliked close calls. Like today.

If he hadn't arrived when he had, he might be processing another crime scene. He didn't know her, but something about this fragile-looking woman stirred him. No, she wasn't fragile, he amended as he recalled the vicious bite she'd given her assailant.

Leila clutched her camera bag close and followed Michaela to his cruiser. The young officer grabbed a blanket from the trunk and handed it to her, then stood outside the vehicle.

Satisfied, he strode to join Carter. He had a murderer to find.

TWO

"The photographer okay?" Carter knelt next to the body, his eyes scanning it. He maintained enough distance so as not to touch the poor woman, even accidentally.

"Yeah," Brett replied. "Shaken up, but I think she's going to be fine. She's got grit."

Carter paused and glanced up with a grin. "That's high praise coming from you."

Brett tucked his thumbs into his belt loops. He recalled the rescue and couldn't keep a smile off his face.

"Did Ryan tell you how she got away from the creep abducting her?" He squatted on the other side of the body. The gentle drizzle beaded on the duct tape. "She bit him. Hard. She actually had his blood on her chin."

"Oh, ick."

"Yeah." The rain stopped playing with them. Now it pelted them in heavy drops. Within minutes, the ground became a swampy mud pit. Leila's pictures would be their strongest evidence in regard to ground markers. Which reminded him…

He called out to Ryan where he and Sergeant Stella Thompson were barricading the area with yellow crime-scene tape. "Make sure you block off the area where we found the camera." The area where Leila had been abducted. He held back a shudder. Why this case bothered him so much, he didn't know. It wasn't his first murder or abduction investigation. And at least in this case, one of the victims survived. That didn't always happen.

"Already on it." Ryan returned to his work.

Brett surveyed his team. All of them were busy, focused on the job. Footsteps approached at a rapid pace. He swiveled to face the incoming officer.

"Lieutenant!" Joe Maillard ran up to them, his face flushed from running. He stopped, fast, nearly skidding into the body.

"Officer!" Brett stood and faced him, glaring. "Never disturb a crime scene."

Carter came to stand beside him, his arms crossed over his chest. He didn't say anything, just silently supported his friend.

Joe's flush darkened until he was as red as the lobsters he used to catch when he was growing up in Maine. "Sorry. I just wanted to tell you, the guy we chased, he got away. He had a car waiting."

"Did you get a good look at it?"

"Yes, sir." Joe's shoulders snapped back. "It was a small SUV. Silver." He rattled off the make and model.

Brett bit back a groan. Those cars were everywhere. "I don't suppose you caught the license plate." It wasn't a question. He could already see the answer in the slump of Joe's shoulders. The younger man gulped.

"No, sir. The entire back end seemed to be covered with mud."

That was common in the area, especially on rainy days if the driver went down bumpy dirt and gravel paths riddled with puddles. Of course, the cynic in Brett found it a little too convenient that this particular car would have its license plate unreadable.

"That's not your fault, Joe. You gave chase, and you took note of what you saw. That's all you could do. Go help Lieutenant Douglass. We need to work quickly before this scene is completely destroyed."

He patted Joe on the shoulder before sending him off to check for any other evidence beyond the trees where they had found Leila's camera. Joe was a fine young officer. He just got a little overzealous at times. He said as much to Carter.

"A few years will season him." Carter shrugged. "We've all been there."

"True enough."

A car pulled up along the curve, directly behind the line of police cars. Brett pushed the button on his shoulder radio. "Chief, the team is still on the scene. The coroner arrived."

"How's the crime scene holding up?" Chief Melody Kaiser's voice floated from the radio.

Brett grimaced. "The rain isn't helping. No one's messed with the body or the area, but if there were any footprints, they're long gone."

The chief sighed. "Keep me posted."

"Will do."

He waited with Carter for the coroner, Deanna Snow. As she passed his cruiser, the door opened and Leila jumped out, leaving her camera bag and supplies in the safety of his vehicle. She carried a single camera with her. Her lips slashed across her face in a flat line.

Michaela followed her. When the young officer looked at Brett, he sighed, then gestured for her to help on the crime scene. She couldn't force Leila to stay in the cruiser.

"Leila!" Deanna started. "Why aren't you over there?"

Leila's mouth softened into a smile. "Hi, Dee. I've finished taking pictures. But I'm very interested in hearing your take on this."

Brett's eyebrows climbed his forehead. The two obviously knew each other, and on more than a professional basis. Leila hadn't told her about her near abduction. Not that there was time for such a discussion.

"You're going to get chilled," he reminded Leila once she and Deanna had approached the body. Leila shrugged and trudged through the puddles forming on the wet ground.

"So's everyone else." She jerked her head to where Michaela stood. Strands of her hair had escaped her bun and were now hanging in a loose group of sodden strings around her pretty face. "I want to know what Dee sees."

"Why? You're not a cop."

She hesitated. "I told you. I don't think this is the real crime scene. Call it professional pride."

But it wasn't. She wasn't telling him everything. She had a deeper reason. He wanted to know what it was.

But there wasn't time to argue. The sky opened and the rain came down in sheets. Everything that hadn't been soaked five minutes earlier was now drenched. He turned away from Leila and strode over to Deanna, aware that the photographer was dogging his steps. She didn't even bother to hide it, splashing through the puddles to keep up with him, her long-legged stride eating up the distance.

"Lieutenant!" Deanna beckoned him closer. She eyed Leila with concern. "Leila, you might not want to see this."

Now he was really curious.

"I've already photographed the body, Dee. I'm good."

Deanna gave in. "Okay. It's your call. Do you see this?" She leaned closer to the corpse and pulled her soggy top away from her shoulder.

He frowned. "Is that a tattoo?"

Beside him, Leila gurgled, a choked, gasping sound.

"What?" Brett glanced around urgently. "You've gone white as a sheet. What's wrong?"

Leila crouched down low to get a better angle. She pointed at the area, her finger trembling like a leaf in a windstorm.

Brett copied her posture.

"That's not a tattoo." She raised tortured eyes and met first his gaze, then Deanna's sympathetic stare. "It's a brand, isn't it?"

"Yes." Deanna nodded. "I'm sorry to say it is. Do you need to get a shot?"

"Oh." Leila fumbled with her camera and zeroed in on the mark to get a better angle. When the camera lowered, her face was even whiter than before.

He froze, his mind catching up to what they were saying. "A brand?"

She nodded, as if unable to speak again.

Brett returned his gaze to the poor woman on the ground. "It can't be him. I'd hoped he was dead."

Leila swallowed. "It's even worse than that. Look at the number."

By now, their conversation had caught the attention of those around them.

"She has a brand?" Officer Witt asked, her words causing a visible wave of revulsion through the ranks of officers. "But the Brand Killer has been silent for years. We haven't had a victim since they found number five. That was over five years ago."

Brett looked at the number. "This brand says number seven."

"So the Brand Killer is back." Carter voiced what he was thinking. "Or we have a copycat on our hands."

"Either way," Leila said, her low voice causing all the murmurs to hush, "we're missing a body. Somewhere, there's a number six."

He suddenly felt like an old man. A family out there was grieving a daughter, not knowing whether she was dead or alive. He wanted to give them closure.

And he wanted to know what Leila's connection to this was. From her reaction, he could tell that she knew far more than she was saying.

"You know something."

Startled, Leila's head shot up. Her eyes collided with a pair of dark blue eyes. Rain dripped from Brett's dark blond military fade and ran in rivulets down his compelling face, too rugged to be Hollywood handsome. But it was definitely the face of someone to trust in times of trouble.

"Leave it for the police station," Deanna told him. "I need to get this poor girl to the morgue so we can find the cause of death."

Leila turned toward her best friend. "She didn't drown?"

"No. She's not bloated enough. I believe she was dead before she hit the water. My guess is asphyxiation, but we'll know soon enough. In the meantime, you know what you need to do."

"Dee—"

"You need to tell them everything. Now that he might be out there again, they need to know."

Dee was right. "I will. I wasn't going to argue," Leila replied.

"Will you follow me?" Brett asked her. "Once we get the scene cleaned up and Deanna gets the body ready to transport to the morgue, we'll head to the station. Is whatever you have to say something the whole team should hear?"

She considered. Her preference would be just him. But then she might have to tell it again. "I think it would be the best way to handle it."

Actually, it would be agony for her, but she refused to let her feelings interfere with doing the right thing.

"Let me grab my stuff from your car, then I'll follow you." She appreciated him not ordering her but asking politely. Although it wasn't like she had a choice. If she refused to speak up, it would be obstruction. Even if she didn't work for the legal system here, she'd still feel honor-bound to tell them what she knew.

But, oh, she dreaded reliving the experience.

It took another twenty minutes to clear everything up. Leila fought back the urge to gag when the body bag was carried past her. *Just like Tara.* She whirled away from the sight, shaking.

"You going to be all right?"

She jumped slightly when Brett appeared at her elbow. She'd been so wrapped up in her own trauma, she hadn't heard him approach. Strangely, his presence steadied her.

"I'm good. I just want to get out of the rain."

"Don't we all. Let's head to the station."

Leila hopped into her SUV and turned the car on. Once it was running, she flipped the heat as high as it would go and turned the heated seats up to the hottest level. She was chilled down to her soul, but whether it was from the rain or the reemergence of her sister's killer, she couldn't say. It was probably a mixture of both.

It seemed to take forever for the heat to kick on. By the time hot air was pumping through the vents, they were pulling into the Sterling Ridge Police Department parking lot.

She climbed out of the car and grabbed her camera equipment. She would never leave that stuff lying around for anyone to mess with. Not only was it valuable, but it contained investigation evidence. She couldn't risk anything being contaminated. Not with the crime scene washed out.

She ran over to meet Brett, and they walked into the station together.

"I called ahead and informed my chief that we had information that everyone needed to hear. She assigned us conference room B."

Leila nodded. "This is my first time here, but I assume it's pretty much like the other departments."

"That's right. I forgot that your contract was new. It's been quite a day."

She understood. Extreme cases made one feel like they had worked together longer. It happened all the time.

Inside the department, she was introduced to the other officers on the team. Finally, she came face-to-face with Chief Melody Kaiser. The chief was smaller than she'd expected, at least three inches below Leila's five-eight. It didn't matter, though. Confidence blazed from the older woman's eyes. She wore her command as comfortably as one would their favorite jacket.

"Leila, would you like anything before you start? Coffee? A soda? Water?"

She really wanted an ice-cold Pepsi, but she'd never sleep tonight if she had caffeine this late in the day. Not that she'd sleep much as it was. She shuddered. Her dreams would be filled with Tara tonight.

Maybe she'd take a sleeping aid.

She recalled the man who'd tried to abduct her and changed her mind. After that, the idea of going into a drugged sleep and not being able to awaken quickly terrified her.

"Just water, please. And may I connect my laptop to your smart board?"

"Of course. Whatever you need to do."

Leila opened her laptop and selected the file she wanted. Joe helped her link it to their system.

Michaela brought her a bottled water from the lunchroom refrigerator and passed it to her with a warm smile.

"Thanks." She took a drink to soothe her suddenly dry throat and then sat in a chair at the middle of the long conference table. Brett took the seat on her right side. The other officers and the chief filled in the rest of the seats until every spot was taken.

One of the officers brought in a box of doughnuts. Michaela took one and passed the box around. When it came to Leila, she looked in and groaned. They were the good kind, topped with chocolate and filled with Bavarian cream. The fresh, sweet scent made her mouth water. She almost took one but didn't think her stomach would tolerate the rich treat at the moment. She passed it on to Brett, who grabbed one and placed it on a napkin in front of him.

She turned away and took a deep breath. Then she began speaking.

"Ten years ago, a young woman was abducted while she was out running. Her family didn't realize she was missing until her twin sister stopped by her apartment and realized she'd never brought in her mail or fed her dog that evening."

She took another sip of water. This was so much harder after believing the killer had died or disappeared. It helped to tell the story as if it pertained to someone else.

"A young family camping found the missing woman's body in a lake three days later. She'd been stabbed multiple times but ultimately died from drowning. The necklace she'd always worn was missing. It was a puzzle necklace.

Each sister had a piece and they fit together to spell their names. Their parents had it made special."

Too much detail. Her throat clogged. She cleared it.

"Her right shoulder had been branded with the number one. The police feared they might have a serial killer. A year later, another body was found. This time, she'd been strangled, and again dumped in the water with a brand on her skin. Three more bodies showed up in the next three years."

Carter leaned his elbows on the table. "The case went cold five or six years ago when no more bodies or leads were found."

She nodded. "I know. Every couple of years, someone looks at the files. But all leads have completely dried up."

"So, is this new girl the victim of a copycat?" Joe asked, raising his hand like a schoolchild.

"You don't think it is." Brett swiveled his chair to look directly at Leila. "You think this is the same killer."

How did he read her so well?

"I do." She toggled the arrow to the next image. Then she brought up a photo of the fifth victim. "Meet Essie Gwyn. Twenty-three. She was taken while out walking her dog. She was found in the water. In fact, the only one not found in the water was today's victim."

Now came the hard part. "All the girls had curly brown hair and brown eyes. All were in their early twenties. All between five-four and five-eight in height."

She pulled up the fourth victim. Then the third. The second.

She paused before pulling up number one. Taking a deep breath, she brought up the image.

When Tara's dead face filled the screen, she gulped. The room went still. She gathered her courage and faced their shocked faces.

"This is Tara Mitchell. She was taken ten years ago on October 15. She had just turned twenty-one. She'd be thirty now, almost thirty-one. She was my identical twin sister."

Leila watched the officers process what she said.

"Leila," Brett said.

She turned to face him. His blank face starkly contrasted with the warm sympathy in his eyes. "Yes?"

"Didn't I hear that you left Sterling Ridge?"

She nodded. "After the third victim was found. My parents sold the house. When there'd been no murders for years, I moved back. That was almost two years ago. I figured it was safe."

She'd been wrong.

The peace her family had left to gain had never materialized. Her mother had been bitter until the day she'd died of cancer. Her father had remarried and all but abandoned Leila. They had both disapproved of Leila's choice to meld her love of photography and her quest for justice. After losing them and her husband, she'd decided to return to Sterling Ridge. She'd told herself she wanted to raise her daughter in the familiar small town she'd grown up in.

But deep inside, she knew she'd come to find out what had really happened to her sister. What she hadn't expected was for the Brand Killer to resurface and begin a new reign of terror after so many years.

THREE

Brett felt as though someone had punched him in the gut. Everyone began talking at once. Mentally, he sorted through everything she'd just told them. All the victims looked very similar. Same build, coloring. In fact… Suddenly, all the air whooshed from his lungs.

"All the victims look like you!" he said.

Immediately, he wished he'd kept his thoughts to himself. Or at least phrased it differently. His colleagues quieted again. As a group, all eyes zeroed in on the forensic photographer, their stares more intense than previously. Leila squirmed at the front of the room under the scrutiny.

Brett met her gaze and grimaced. *Sorry*, he mouthed. She jerked her chin in acknowledgment before responding to his comment.

"Yeah, I noticed that. Or rather, I noticed that they all looked like Tara, since she was his victim. He never came after me."

"Why'd he stop for so many years, then kill again?" Ryan asked around a mouthful of doughnut.

Brett watched her for a second more, then refocused on the case. He'd ask her for more details when they got a moment alone. He needed more information. In a case like this, even the most seemingly unimportant fact could lead to a break in the case.

"I don't know why he stopped. I hoped—everyone thought—that the Brand Killer had probably died. There have been no other cases in other parts of the country, so he didn't move on, at least not that we're aware of. Serial killers don't usually stop or get over their compulsion to kill."

Her comment told him that even though her family had relocated to find peace, she hadn't moved on. Not completely. She'd still watched for TBK, as the press had dubbed the killer. Probably even had alerts set on her phone to let her know of any mentions of the killer on the internet. That's what he'd do.

"Obviously he didn't die. But he did stop for about five years. All the leads had gone cold." Brett twirled a pen in his fingers like a small baton.

"Until now." Leila pushed a brown curl behind her ear. Two small earrings twinkled at him.

Again he had the feeling she was withholding information. He leaned closer to her. "Is there something you're not telling us?"

Why was he so careful about her feelings? This was a murder investigation.

"Not anything related to the case," she whispered back, keeping her eyes ahead. "It's personal. I don't mind telling you later, just in case, but I don't think it has anything to do with the killer."

He let it drop. He'd be a hypocrite if he demanded she spill her secrets. He had some baggage of his own. Stuff only Carter knew. Who was he to throw stones?

"Is there anything else we need to know, Leila?" Chief Kaiser's voice silenced the others.

"I don't think so."

"Are you in danger?" Sergeant Stella Thompson asked, her brow furrowed. "After all, you are exactly his type."

Leila's face flushed. "Again, I don't think so. All the other victims were in their early twenties, so much younger than I am."

"He did try to abduct you," Joe said, pushing his glasses up his nose.

"The kid has a point." Brett lifted an eyebrow. He did not like the direction this was taking. Was Leila still in danger?

"I thought about that on the way over. I think maybe I was taken because I stumbled onto his hiding spot. He clearly had set it up so he could watch the cops find the body. Kind of like a gotcha to show he was back."

Brett wasn't convinced. Even though she was older than the others, she still looked young enough to be a target.

"I wonder if the Brand Killer knew any of the victims." Michaela stood and helped herself to another doughnut.

He still hadn't touched the pastry he'd grabbed. Leila kept eyeing it. Maybe she regretted not taking a doughnut but was too well-mannered to ask for one. Not too timid. There was nothing timid about Leila. She might be secretive, but he'd already witnessed the fierce side of her.

"Your last name is different than your sister's. I assume you're married?" the chief remarked.

Brett froze. Married. She was thirty. And pretty. Why wouldn't an intelligent lady like her be married?

She gulped down a sip of water, spluttering slightly. The question must have caught her off guard.

"Um, widowed."

Ouch. That was hard.

"I'm sorry to hear that," the chief said.

"It's okay. You didn't know. And he's been gone for several years now."

The door opened and Deanna Snow stepped into the room. "Is it okay if I join you? I'd like to share my findings."

Chief Kaiser motioned for her to enter. "Please. We just finished talking about the history of the Brand Killer. The general consensus seems to be it's very possible that it's actually him and not a copycat. I'll need the team to go over the case with a fine-toothed comb. See if there's anything that our new technology can add to this."

Deanna moved to the computer that Leila had used. Leila gestured for her to go ahead. After all, her computer was already hooked up to the Smart Board. Deanna attached a thumb drive and opened it up, then shared it with the room. The image showed the brand on victim number one. Leila's sister.

Leila's hands clenched on the table. Brett tapped her foot with his. Not to tell her to stop, but to let her know he was there to support her. She dipped her head a fraction then stilled.

Deanna didn't look her way, and the other officers took her lead, giving Leila time to regain her composure.

"See the bottom of the mark?" the coroner asked.

Brett narrowed his gaze and leaned in. He'd never noticed before that the odd squiggle was anything more than a blurred image. "Is that a petal?"

"Yep. It's a flower. Every victim had it, but it's not always in the same place." She brought up an image from the internet. It was an odd flower, one he'd never seen before, with three petals that seemed to have weird tentacles at the end of each one.

"It looks like one of those flesh-eating plants."

He nodded at Ryan's words. "Now that you mention it, it does."

"It's called a monkey orchid. It means charm and playfulness but can also be used to symbolize evil and death. Whoever this Brand Killer is, he somehow embossed this flower into each and every brand. Including the body we found today."

For whatever reason, the Brand Killer had returned. Brett scanned the room, meeting the gaze of every police officer. In each one he saw the same steely determination.

No matter what it took, they would find this killer and bring him to justice.

He was really back.

Leila leaped to her feet, nearly tipping her chair over in her haste.

"Leila! What's going on?" Brett rose to his feet, his hands out in a calming motion.

"He's back. Please. I need to go home. I need to check on my daughter." It wasn't rational, she knew it, but her heart hammered in her chest. She rubbed it, trying to ease the discomfort.

"We understand, Leila." Chief Kaiser walked around the table and took her hand. "Go home. Get some rest. Lieutenant Talbot?"

"Ma'am."

"Please follow Leila home and check out her residence. I know the likelihood of the killer going after Leila is slim, but let's not tempt it, shall we?"

Normally, Leila would have protested that she was perfectly capable of seeing herself home. Except right now, she wasn't. In fact, she'd welcome the presence of the stern police lieutenant with his quiet, take-charge attitude and gravelly voice. If for no other reason than to protect Evie.

She didn't wait around to talk with Dee or to chitchat with any of the officers. She practically ran out of the station to her vehicle.

"Leila." She stopped outside her car and flicked her eyes

to Brett. "I'll follow you. When we get to your house, I'll look it over. Is your daughter at your house?"

She unlocked her car door. They were taking too long. Thankfully, the rain had passed. Otherwise she'd be soaked all over again. "Yes. I have a babysitter who stays with her while I work. She doesn't have a car, so normally I either drive her home or she stays the night."

"Why don't you call her?"

"She's Amish. She doesn't have a phone and doesn't usually answer the landline." After today, she'd insist on the latter. Katie would not argue. It was for work, and not in her own house, after all.

"Give me your cell phone number, and your address, just in case I lose you."

She bit back an impatient growl and exchanged numbers. Then she gave him her address and watched him bring up a map to her house on his phone. What he asked made sense, she knew it did. She just hated the time it took to accomplish it.

"That should do it." Brett pocketed his phone and jogged over to his cruiser.

Finally. Leila hopped in her SUV and started the ignition. She didn't wait to see if Brett was in his cruiser before she jerked the gearshift into Reverse and backed out of her parking space.

Be safe, she reminded herself. *Always take care of yourself first.* If she got into an accident, she couldn't help her daughter.

It took every ounce of self-control she possessed to drive at the posted speed limit. Several times, she had to tap the brakes to bring her speed down to accepted parameters. She glanced in her rearview mirror. No flashing lights. Apparently, Brett was going to ignore her traffic violations in favor of making sure her daughter was safe.

The light ahead of her turned yellow. "Ugh!"

She knew she'd never make it, so she stopped and clenched her fingers around the steering wheel.

Her phone rang. It was Brett. She jabbed the button on her dashboard to answer. "Yes?"

"GPS says there's an accident within the next mile."

She bit back her panic. "What's the fastest route?"

She should know this, but she'd never needed to get home from this station before today.

"Follow me." He hung up and his siren went on. Immediately, the traffic around them slowed. He swerved past her, waited for the cars to cross the intersection and moved his vehicle into the space, blocking oncoming traffic.

Her heart swelled with gratitude. He'd made it so she could go through the light. The moment she crossed the intersection, he zoomed up ahead of her and led her through the streets of Sterling Ridge until they arrived at Aspen Lane, where she and her daughter had lived since she'd moved back, a widow shattered by her husband's sudden and scandalous death.

He pulled up to her house and parked on the street, then he turned off the lights and siren. Leila whipped her car into the driveway and jumped out. Brett arrived at the front door a mere ten seconds before her.

The door swung open. Katie Weaver stood there, blinking at the tall police officer on the front step.

"Katie…" Leila huffed. She pulled out her inhaler and shook it before inhaling the medicine. The tightness in her chest eased. "Where's Evie? Is she okay?"

"*Ja*. She's *gut*. I just fed her dinner." She backed away from the door to let Brett and Leila enter.

"This is Lieutenant Brett Talbot. He's going to check out the house and maybe look around the yard. Just to be sure."

Katie clearly didn't understand, but she didn't argue. Leila went to the living room, where Evie sat watching her favorite cartoon.

"Mommy!" The child flung herself into her mother's arms with carefree exuberance, completely unaware of any danger. Leila hugged her daughter, kissing her head. She held her tight for a few moments, and her body stopped trembling.

"Leila."

She turned, her baby still in her arms, and smiled at Brett, her heart full.

He smiled back. "Hey. I looked through your house. Not hard, since you only have one floor."

She stepped away from her daughter and walked over to him. "I'm assuming you didn't find anything."

"I didn't. Look, I'm going to search the backyard. If everything's clear, I'll give Katie a ride home for you. Then I'll be back."

She hated being a bother. "Oh, you don't have to."

He shook his head. "I think I do. I know you said you didn't think you were in danger, but, Leila, this guy set up a crime scene for us to find. I think that you being the sister of the first victim, and having just signed on with our department, is odd. It feels off to me. Too coincidental."

She swallowed. She'd avoided dwelling on the details too closely, but hadn't she thought the same thing?

"Okay. Whatever you need to do."

A few minutes later, he left to take Katie home.

Leila carried on with her normal evening ritual of getting Evie ready for bed. The little girl picked out two books.

They snuggled on the bed together while Leila read them. When she finished, she set the books aside.

"Sing to me, Mommy." Happy to oblige, she sang one song, then kissed Evie's cheek.

"Good night, sweetheart. Mommy will see you in the morning."

She pulled the door behind her, leaving it open a couple of inches so she'd hear if Evie woke up. Where was Brett? Not that it was necessary for him to come back. After all, he'd checked the house. She was here to watch her daughter, and all the locks were fastened.

She wandered into the bedroom and flipped on her light. A necklace lay on the large decorative pillow on her bed. A necklace that hadn't been there an hour ago. One she hadn't seen for over ten years, not since the Brand Killer had removed it from her sister's neck.

He'd been in her house.

Leila opened her mouth and screamed. The scream was cut off when strong arms grabbed her from behind.

"Scream again and the little girl dies with you."

Her baby. Please, God, she prayed, let Brett come and save them.

FOUR

One of the arms holding her tight briefly released her. She'd barely registered the fact before it snaked around her throat, pulling her back against a muscular chest. Her captor's bicep tightened around her neck, squeezing her airway. A strangled wheeze escaped her lips. She scratched at the arm, her short nails ineffectively scraping the leather jacket he wore. Her lungs burned. She was going to suffocate.

Then relief hit when he loosened his grip. The edge of panic eased a degree. Since Tara's death, Leila had developed an intense fear of drowning or suffocating. Now Leila forced herself to think. She couldn't give in to the terror building up in her soul. Not if she wanted Evie and herself to survive this ordeal.

"Do you hear me?" he snarled in her ear. "Do not scream."

She nodded. His hold tightened painfully again. He wanted to hear the words. She forced the words through her aching throat. "I understand."

She wouldn't put her daughter in danger. She wouldn't scream. But neither would she accept her death at the hands of a monster so easily. Brett. He would return soon. If she could stay alive and keep this creep occupied until then, Brett would save them. The assailant wouldn't have time to deal with her, hurt Evie and take on the lawman.

"Good. We're going to move to the window. I have plans for you."

Leila couldn't stop the shudder that racked through her. Her captor laughed softly. It was a pleasant laugh, one that would have made her smile if she'd heard it in public. Now it made her stomach churn.

He began to drag her toward the window. Her room wasn't a large one. Only a few feet separated her from the window. She could see the curtains billowing in the breeze and knew exactly how this man had entered her home. And now he planned to take her out the same way so he could kill her.

Just like he'd killed Tara and six other unsuspecting women.

Leila refused to be victim number eight.

He tugged her along. Even with her feet scraping the ground, she couldn't keep him from closing in on the window.

The safety she'd once felt in moving out of an apartment and into a house vanished like a puff of smoke.

Oh, no. Once they left the house, Brett might never find her. She couldn't let him take her away. But what could she do about it? He was so much stronger than she was. Plus, her head barely came up to his throat. If he had been shorter, she would throw her head back and try to break his nose. Leila curved her fingers into claws and tried to dig at his eyes. She met with some kind of fabric. Obviously, his face was covered. He growled in her ear and tightened his grip around her throat again. She was not going to be strangled in her own home. Deliberately, Leila stumbled. The weight of her body falling sideways loosened his hold on her. She dropped to her knees and whirled around to face him.

As she'd suspected, he wore a mask over his face. A ghoulish Grim Reaper one like she'd see in the stores around Halloween. Except this one was made of cloth and appeared to be homemade. It completely covered his head. Even his eyes were concealed. But why? He planned to kill her, which would mean she wouldn't be around to tell anyone.

Then he chuckled again.

She shivered.

"You're still feisty."

Still? The horror of the implication hit her like a baseball bat to the stomach. For a moment, she forgot how to breathe. When spots formed in her vision, she gasped in a huge gulp of air.

"Oh, yes. I didn't know you had a twin. It was a shame, that." He shrugged. "Too bad. Your time has run out." He lunged for her, yanking her up by her arms. His long fingers dug into her flesh, despite the long-sleeved shirt she had on. She wiggled to increase the distance between them. It was no use. She was no match for his strength.

Leila struggled, twisting and flailing in his grasp. She didn't scream, though, protecting her daughter still foremost in her thoughts.

Nothing she did worked. He hauled her to the window as if she was no more than a child. He straddled the windowsill and tugged her closer.

Once he sat, though, he'd lost the advantage his height had given him. Leila stomped on his foot. He growled. She slipped a few inches away. He leaned forward to grab her again. This time, the hard heel of her boot connected with his shin. Her attacker howled and fell forward into the room.

Leila spun away from him. His long arms reached out and snagged her ankle. She slammed against the sharp edge of the dresser, catching herself before she toppled over and onto the ground. When he lunged for her again, she lost her balance completely and hit the floor. She rolled to her hands and knees and crawled away from him as fast as she could, ignoring the discomfort to her knees against the solid wood floor.

"You're not getting away from me." He spat a derogatory word at her.

She ignored it. At that moment, she heard the best sound she had ever heard: a car pulling into the driveway. She heard the engine cut off and a door open. It had to be Brett. People rarely visited her. The only friends she had were Dee and Katy.

Her assailant stood and made another grab for her. Leila ducked out of his reach, sucked in a lungful of air and screamed.

"Brett!"

Scrambling away, she sprang to her feet. But she wasn't fast enough. Her assailant slammed her against the wall. She was face-to-face with that horrible mask for a second before fingers closed around her neck, cutting off her air supply. She choked.

Would Brett get to her in time?

Brett leaped from his cruiser, Leila's scream still echoing in his mind. His gaze shot to the house. From where he stood, he couldn't see anything, but he knew terror when he heard it.

Charging toward the front door, he tried the knob. When it wouldn't turn, he stepped back and kicked it in. The heavy wood splintered and swung in, banging against the inside wall.

He raced into the house. "Leila!"

Shuffling noises to the right alerted him. He flattened

himself against the outside wall leading to the room. Hand on his weapon, he slid along the wall and peeked into Leila's room. His blood ran cold. A man in a mask held Leila against the wall next to a wide-open window, his hands around her bare throat. Leila struggled, but weakly.

Brett jumped in through the door, his Glock out and ready.

"Stop! Police! Release her and step away."

Leila's assailant jerked his hands away from her neck. Brett aimed his Glock at him, but the attacker shoved Leila, who was holding her throat and coughing, at the lawman.

Leila spun in his direction. When she stumbled, Brett caught her in his arms. Momentum nearly brought them both to the ground. Brett shifted his weight, keeping them balanced and upright, but it was a close call. His gaze shot across the room in time to see the assailant dive out the window.

Instinctively, Brett made a move to charge after him. However, the quivering woman in his arms began falling the instant he let her go. He grabbed her again.

"Easy. I won't let you fall."

She shook her head. "Go," she gasped at him, her voice rough and raw, as if she'd inhaled smoke. "I'm fine. Catch him."

Brett steered Leila to the bed and gently settled her on the edge. Carefully, he removed his arms until he no longer supported her weight. She slumped but stayed seated. Her one hand grabbed her inhaler from her pocket. Satisfied that she wouldn't collapse, he ran to the window.

The man who had tried to strangle her was nowhere in sight. Nor could Brett see any signs of him from his position. That didn't mean there wouldn't be signs on the ground. But with only the light of the moon, it was hard to tell. He needed eyes on the ground to conduct a proper check. But Brett refused to leave this woman and her child unguarded.

The child.

Brett spun to face her. "Your daughter?"

She was on her feet and out the door in a flash.

Brett caught up with her. They reached the next bedroom and Leila peered in before leaning weakly against the wall. In the glow of a princess night-light, Evie slept peacefully, her tiny arms wrapped around a stuffed unicorn. Even as they watched, she snuggled deeper into her pillow.

She was fine.

With that assurance, Brett turned his mind back to his other duties. And to finding the killer who had nearly finished off Leila. What if he'd returned from driving Katie home five minutes later? Even two minutes would have been too late. A vision of Leila's pale face and unseeing eyes seared his brain.

No. He could not think of that now. Resolutely, he shoved the thoughts aside and reached for his phone. He dialed Chief Kaiser. His boss picked up on the second ring.

"Chief Kaiser here." His superior's calm voice steadied him.

"Chief, it's Lieutenant Talbot. We've had an incident. Someone—and I have to assume it was the same man who attacked Leila at the crime scene—invaded Leila's home and attempted to kill her. The attacker fled before I could apprehend him. I need backup and the crime scene unit."

Brett walked back to Evie's door and checked on Leila. She remained seated at her daughter's bedside. She looked up and saw him. After kissing the top of her daughter's head, she softly made her way to him. Brett stepped out of the doorway so she had room to join him in the hallway.

"Does she need an ambulance?" Chief Kaiser asked.

Brett cast a glance at Leila. She shook her head.

"I'm fine," she said. Her voice was still rough around the edges, but it was stronger than it had been before.

He wasn't completely convinced. Bruises already darkened the skin around her neck. The rest of her face remained unnaturally pale. That decided him.

"I don't think a paramedic to check her over would be bad idea."

Leila frowned at him, her eyes slitting to a narrow glare. That she was clearly unhappy with him didn't matter. He was more concerned about her well-being. He would do whatever he needed to do to keep her safe.

"How is the child?" The chief broke into their silent battle of wills.

"Unharmed," he responded. "We checked on her before I called you. It seems the attacker entered through the window in Leila's room and waited for her there."

Leila shivered and rubbed her hands up her arms. He shook off the impulse to comfort her. She didn't know him. No matter what his intent, that kind of invasion of her personal space would not be welcomed. Or appropriate.

"Very good. Backup is on the way, Lieutenant."

Brett thanked the chief and ended the call.

Leila stepped closer to him. The hallway fixture hit the bruises with an unflattering light.

"Does your throat hurt?"

She rubbed the area, wincing. "It's tender. Though, honestly, I think the way I screamed could have caused that."

"How did Evie sleep through that?"

She chuckled.

"How can you find humor in any of this?"

"I'm not laughing at the situation. I'm laughing because

you don't know Evie. She sleeps through everything. Thunderstorms. Cars backfiring."

He allowed a small smile. "That will be fun when you have to wake her up early to get ready for school."

"Not looking forward to it."

Brett glanced at his phone to check the time. It was almost nine in the evening. "I will wait for backup and the crime scene unit to arrive. I don't want to leave you and Evie alone until then. Once they're here, we'll check around and see if there are any clues."

She nodded, but her eyes never left the sleeping form of her little girl.

Flashing lights outside alerted him to the arrival of his team. Thankfully, they had not come in with sirens blaring. Brett met them at the front door.

"Officer Witt, I want you to stay inside with Leila and her daughter just in case our guy hasn't gone as far away as we think."

"Yes, sir." The young officer disappeared inside the house.

He turned to the three other officers. "I want this entire block checked. Start with the immediate area surrounding the house. Leave no bush or tree or shed unchecked. We can't take the chance that he will go after anyone. Then spread out."

Within minutes, the officers had their flashlights out and a full sweep commenced. Despite the fact that the killer's footprints might be disrupted, they had to chase while the trail was fresh.

The members of the crime scene unit arrived and immediately started setting up tape around the area. Which made sense. Whoever had attacked Leila could have left fingerprints.

Brett returned inside.

He stopped, blinking, when he saw Leila waiting for him beyond the door, Evie sleeping on her shoulder.

"Are you going somewhere?"

She snorted softly. "My bedroom has been broken into, and my house is a crime scene. I can't stay here while they sort it out."

That was true. "Where will you stay?"

"I'll head for the motel in town. They should have a room."

"I'll send Michaela in with you so you can pack a bag without messing up the crime scene. The team is still dusting for prints."

"No need. I always keep a bag packed for myself and Evie. Just in case I'm called out at a late hour. I never planned to be called out for a crime at my own house, though. That was never on my radar."

He appreciated her attempt to keep the mood light, but he could see the fear lingering in her eyes. Her complexion remained pale.

"Before you go to the motel, you should give your statement. The sooner we have all the details, the sooner we can put this guy away. How about this? I'll drive you to the station to get your official statement. My officers will interview the neighbors and let us know if they find anything. When we're done, I'll take you to the motel myself. I'm sure the chief will want to provide you with protection."

She nodded but didn't look too hopeful. He couldn't imagine what a horror this must be for her.

FIVE

Before they could leave, the paramedics arrived. Although Leila protested that she was fine, Brett insisted she get checked out. She huffed and gave in. It was obvious he planned on being stubborn. Both paramedics trailed her when she stalked to the kitchen. She dragged out a chair and sat at the kitchen table through the paramedic's examination, her nerves taut. The house that had always felt so safe now felt like it was closing in on her. Leila didn't often feel claustrophobic—she avoided most closed-in spaces—but she was feeling that way now. Only the presence of Brett leaning against the kitchen counter kept her from leaping to her feet. The moment the paramedics left, she stood, shaking her arms to rid herself of the itchy sensation crawling over her skin. What she needed now was to keep busy.

She also needed to tell Brett what her attacker had said to her. Not now, though. Too many ears. And she couldn't relive the ordeal in her home.

"What now?" She glanced at Brett.

He pushed away from the countertop. "Let's head to the station. The team will finish up here. I called the chief. She's waiting for us."

Leila winced. "Shouldn't she be home by now?"

He shrugged. "She wanted to know what was going on."

At the police station, one of the officers had set up a cot with a pillow and blanket in the smaller conference room. Leila carried Evie, still sound asleep, into the room and settled her on the cot with her toy unicorn.

"We can go right next door," Brett whispered.

"There's no need to whisper," she told him in an almost normal speaking voice. "I told you, she'll sleep through anything."

"Okay. Let's go."

Leila bit her lip to hold in a smile. He still whispered. Some habits were hard to break. She joined him at the door, then turned back and froze. Evie looked so tiny and vulnerable in the strange space.

"Leila?"

"What if she wakes up, Brett? She'll be scared, all by herself."

His brow furrowed. Not in irritation. He looked like he was thinking. "Hold on one minute."

Brett strode away and disappeared around the corner. He moved quietly for a man who had to be six feet tall, all of it muscle. She didn't stray from the doorway. Brett returned a moment later, Officer Witt in tow.

Leila hadn't realized she'd returned to the station with them.

The young woman slipped into the room and set up her laptop on the conference table, along with a large travel mug.

"I asked Michaela come back to the station in case we needed someone to stay with your daughter. She will remain with Evie while we talk. If your daughter stirs, she'll let us know immediately."

His kindness touched her heart. Leila still hated leaving her daughter, but she knew it was the best she could expect. The coming conversation wasn't one she wanted the four-year-old to overhear.

She smiled at the young officer.

"Thanks, Michaela. I appreciate your help."

"It's my pleasure. Don't worry. She will be fine with me. I'm the oldest of five kids. I've logged in lots of hours babysitting."

Leila smiled tightly, then followed Brett into the larger conference room next door. The chief sat at the rectangular table. She rose when Leila and Brett entered.

"Did you get the child settled in?"

"Yes, thank you," Leila replied. "Sorry that you had to come in. I know you're probably supposed to be off duty."

Chief Kaiser waved away the apology. "I'll go home after we talk. I don't like leaving when one of our own needs me."

A lump formed in Leila's throat, surprising her. It had been a long time since she felt like she belonged anywhere. To hear this woman claim her as part of her police family, even though they had only met earlier that day, humbled her.

She'd embarrass herself if she tried to speak, so Leila merely nodded in response. She joined the other two at the table.

"Can I get you anything before we begin?" the chief asked. "Water or coffee?"

"Or a Pepsi?" Brett added. "I noticed you had some at your house."

"No, thanks." She held out her hand. It still shook a little. "Any more caffeine and I'd really have the jitters. Water would be fine."

Brett stood and went to the door. He asked a passing officer to bring a cold bottle of water to the room. When it arrived, he handed it to her. She took a sip to calm her nerves.

"Let's start from what happened after you left here," the chief said.

"Brett followed me to my house. He checked it out, pretty thoroughly. I didn't see anything suspicious at the time. Did you?" She glanced his way.

Brett jumped in. "Right. There was no sign of any forced entry or anyone else on the premises at the time. I recall that all the windows were locked."

Leila agreed. "Yeah. I checked them, too, after you left to drive Katie home."

"Katie?" The chief looked up from her notes.

"My babysitter. She's an Amish woman who cares for Evie while I'm at work. Brett, you weren't gone that long."

"Less than thirty minutes. I dropped her off, then came right back to your place. I opened the door of my cruiser and heard you scream. I, uh, I am sorry I kicked in your front door. You'll need to get it replaced."

"No problem." He could have knocked down an entire wall and she wouldn't care. He'd saved them. Would she ever be able to live in that house again? The memory of her near-death experience would forever be linked to her bedroom.

She shivered. "I had put Evie to bed. When I went back into my room, something felt off."

She couldn't stay in her seat. Shoving back her chair, she stood and paced while she talked. "Remember that I told you my parents had given Tara and me puzzle-piece necklaces?"

"Yeah?" Brett's posture straightened.

"Tara's killer took hers. But tonight it was sitting on my

bed. When I turned…" She looped her arms around her waist to hold off the tremors rumbling through her body.

Then Brett was there, his hands warm and solid on her shoulders. "Easy, Leila. Take a deep breath."

His warmth seeped into her. She closed her eyes and described the man who attacked her.

"I'll have the team find the necklace and bag it for evidence." He grabbed his phone and tapped out a text.

She used those few seconds to compose herself. Her loss of control embarrassed her. Whatever was happening, she was a professional and needed to act the part. She dropped her arms to her side and returned to the table, although she didn't resume her seat. She could act calmer if she remained standing.

Brett's phone dinged. "Rick says he has the necklace. When they're done there, he'll have it delivered to evidence."

"When it's cleared, and this is done, can I have it back?"

It wouldn't bring Tara back to her, but she knew it wouldn't hold any meaning for anyone but her or her dad. If her dad still recalled that he'd once had twin daughters.

She tore her mind from her absent father.

"Sure," the chief responded. "Anything else you can tell us now before we call it a day?"

"I think the killer was someone I knew."

Both Brett and the chief went still.

"Oh? Why do you think that?" The chief leaned forward.

"When he was in my room, before he tried to strangle me, he told me he hadn't known I had a twin. And that I was still feisty."

The horror of those words hit her again. Her sister's death had been a mistake. Leila had been the real target. She fought the urge to vomit. If this was someone she knew, had she missed some clue, failed to notice a sign that someone in her midst was a potential serial killer?

Could she have saved Tara's life?

"Don't go there."

"Huh?" She frowned at Brett.

"You're blaming yourself for your sister's death, aren't you?" He folded his arms across his chest and leaned back in his chair.

She shrugged one shoulder. "I don't know. I just feel like maybe there was more than I could have done."

"Like what? You can't change anything."

She sighed and collapsed back into her chair. He was right. She knew he was. It didn't help her now.

Especially since the killer seemed intent on correcting his original mistake.

Brett didn't like the expression on Leila's face. She'd already been pale. Now her skin had taken on a grayish tint.

Was she going into shock? Severe trauma, even if it was only emotional, could cause that to happen. He'd seen it in his years as a police officer.

When her gaze met his, her eyes were steady. He relaxed back in his chair.

"Why is he coming after me now?" she asked him. "And was that woman killed this morning someone who would have died anyway, or was he trying to lure me out?"

"We can't assume his motives. For all we know, he could have just wanted us to know he was back. I can't imagine he expected you to go searching the woods alone."

The more he thought about it, though, the less he liked it. He had more questions than answers.

"For now, I think we have to assume that you're in danger." Chief Kaiser stood. "I think it's unlikely that he planned on you coming back. After all, we didn't receive the notification that you were our new forensic photographer until this morning. According to the coroner's report, our victim had been dead since yesterday."

"Has she been identified yet?" Leila's question should have been commonplace, but Brett heard the layer of pain woven through her voice. She'd lived what the victim's family was experiencing.

"Not yet."

His phone rang. He checked the display and read the name.

"It's Rick Bruce. The crime scene unit's lead investigator at your house." He swiped his finger across his screen to accept the call. "Yeah, Rick. What do you have?"

"Hey, Brett. None of the neighbors noticed anything out of the ordinary. They didn't know anything was happening until the lady across the street heard Leila scream."

Brett put the phone on speaker and set it on the table. "So the neighbor heard Leila scream? Did she call 911?"

He didn't recall another call coming through.

"No. She'd seen your cruiser pull in the driveway and figured you had it covered."

Leila snickered.

"What?"

"My neighbor is nosy. She's always watching the goings-on."

"Well," Rick said, "she didn't see your intruder. Anyway, the only sign of forced entry was the bedroom window. The screen had been ripped out and the lock broken. Leila, I suggest you have all the locks replaced. The ones on the windows are all pretty cheap and easy to break."

"I'll do it immediately," she murmured.

"I didn't catch that."

"Leila agreed with you," Brett said.

The phone call ended a few seconds later.

"I've been thinking about what you said." He shifted to stretch his legs out in front of him. Some days, especially when the barometric pressure changed, his knee ached. An old wrestling injury that had mostly healed, but never quite regained all its elasticity. "Is it possible that the killer was a stalker and not necessarily someone you knew? I'd expect anyone who talked with you long enough would have learned you had a twin sister."

She took a small sip of her water. "Hmm. I see what you're saying. I never noticed anyone stalking me, but I guess it's possible. I almost wish it were someone I'd met, so we could really narrow down the field of suspects."

"I'm not saying you've never met him. But now that you have faced him, did anything about the guy strike you as familiar?"

She shook her head. "Absolutely not. I couldn't see his face through that mask. I do remember thinking I'd have remembered that laugh, if nothing else. But I didn't recognize that or his voice."

Chief Kaiser rose to her feet in a single, fluid motion. "I think this is all that can be accomplished this evening. Leila, do you have anywhere to stay? Any family nearby?"

Leila squirmed and ducked her head. "We'll be fine."

Which meant no. She'd mentioned a motel, but he was even less a fan of that idea than he'd been earlier.

"Leila?"

She tossed her head. "Look, I'm sure we can find a place for the next night or two. I was planning on going to a motel, at least for tonight."

The chief frowned. "I think we need to come up with another idea."

Brett nodded. "I agree." He held out a hand when she opened her mouth as if to interrupt him. "Now that I know this was someone who had known you in some way, I don't feel comfortable dropping you off somewhere."

"Brett's right. I don't know if we have the necessary personnel to protect you and Evie at a motel, search for the killer and find out who victim number seven is. We are also searching for victim number six." Chief Kaiser ticked each item off on her fingers.

At this reminder of all that was at stake, Leila's shoulders slumped. Briefly, her hands covered her face. When she removed them, grief and determination were carved into her features. "You're right. I know you're right. But I'm not sure where else we can go. The only family I have left is my father, and he lives in Colorado. I haven't spoken with him in over two years."

Brett scratched his neck. "That's too bad. I mean it. But maybe you could still call him…"

She shook her head. "I will not go to Colorado. This person—" she spat the word "—disrupted our lives before. It took years to recover. I will not put my life on hold for him again. I have a job to do, and I intend to do it."

There were so many reasons to persuade her to leave and pay her dad a visit. She was in danger. She was too close to the case. They had no idea how long it could drag on.

But he remembered when his father had gone too far. The social workers tried to remove Brett from the area. To stop him from being there for his mom during her last days.

If they had convinced him to leave, he would have never gotten the closure he'd had holding her hand while she died. He'd never have been in the courtroom when his abusive father had been sentenced to life in prison.

None of those situations had been pleasant, but he'd

needed them to put his past behind him and move on with his life. How could he deny Leila the same privilege?

"I still don't like having you at a hotel or motel where anyone could sneak in," he mused. "What if we could find a place with a little more security?"

The door opened and Michaela entered the room, leading Evie, who clung to her hand. The little girl's quivering pout and tearstained cheeks melted his heart. Her stuffed unicorn dangled from her clenched fingers.

"Evie! I'm right here." Leila rushed over and dropped to her knees before her daughter. The child flung her arms around her mother, the unicorn thumping across Leila's back. "Honey, you're fine. Did you have a bad dream?"

"I waked up, Mommy, and I wasn't in my bed. I called you, but you didn't come."

"I brought her as soon as she called for you," Michaela informed her. "I told you your mom was right next door, didn't I, pumpkin?"

Evie nodded her head against Leila's shoulder. "But I didn't seen her."

Despite the pathos in her voice and the harsh circumstances, Brett chuckled. Kid grammar cracked him up.

"Hey, Michaela, I don't suppose you have room for a couple of houseguests for a day or two?" Until the words came out of his mouth, he thought he was making a joke. But it might be a decent solution to their problem. Michaela lived alone now that her roommate had recently married and moved out. She'd been searching for a new one but so far hadn't found anyone she felt comfortable sharing with.

Michaela flashed a surprised glance at him. "Sir?"

The chief also looked at him before nodding once. "This is not an order, Officer. You are free to refuse. But if you do have room, we need to find a place for Leila and her daughter to stay because her house is a crime scene. Also, it seems that TBK has a personal vendetta against her."

At the moniker *TBK*, Michaela's face hardened. "No problem, Chief. Sir. Leila and the kiddo here can bunk with me as long as they need to. The only issue is what to do when I'm at work."

"We can provide some protection," the chief assured her. "It's easier at a single home than at a hotel with people moving in and out."

"My babysitter—"

Brett turned to Leila. "Do you think Katie would be okay with it if someone picked her up in the morning and dropped her off each evening when you get home from work?"

"I don't see why she wouldn't be. She's very flexible. She has to be with my schedule."

While not completely convinced, Leila seemed to be accepting the inevitable. She couldn't return to her own home, not yet.

"Someone will have to explain the change to her when she's picked up in the morning. I'm assuming you don't want me to go and do it?"

Brett leaned back in his chair. "I don't think so. For the time being, I want to make sure you are secure. And if she does have qualms about the change, we'll have to come up with a new plan."

"Fine. Fine."

"I'm never comfortable when a woman says something is fine." He chuckled when she narrowed her eyes. "Am I wrong?"

"I'll admit nothing about this situation is ideal. But I can't do anything about it. And you are trying to help, so I can't complain." She kissed Evie's cheek before looking around and meeting their eyes. Brett hated how tired she looked. "I am grateful. Thank you all for your help."

As if they were simply assisting her in completing a project or carrying groceries.

It amazed him, the way some people could take on burdens and weather storms with such grace. His mind went again to his mother, who had crumpled when things started going wrong.

No. It was wrong to compare the two women. The challenges they faced were completely different.

He made himself a promise. Now that he was involved with this case, and now that he had seen how much danger Leila and her daughter were in, he would make it his mission to make sure Leila and her precious little girl didn't wind up dead—like his mother had.

SIX

Despite the exhaustion weighing him down, Brett tossed and turned for hours. At midnight, he stomped out of his room and went downstairs to run on the treadmill, hoping the physical activity would wear him out so he could sleep. He could not switch his mind off. The image of a person in a creepy mask strangling Leila flashed in his mind every time he closed his eyes.

For the first time in years, he was tempted to take a sleeping aid. He resisted the temptation. Those things bothered him. What if he missed the alarm? Or what if it affected how he performed his duty the next day?

Granted, not being able to sleep was going to affect his duty, too. No doubt about it. But he could always up his caffeine intake.

After a half-hour run, he showered again and headed back to bed.

Finally, around two in the morning, he drifted off into a restless sleep. When his alarm went off at six, he groaned before flipping the covers back and getting out of bed. He might be tired, but he still had a job to do. He did his morning devotions. When he put his Bible back on the shelf, he decided to skip his morning run. He'd already gotten some exercise just a few hours earlier.

This was going to be long day. He needed sustenance. He padded in his socks to the kitchen to make a large pot of coffee, then, after dressing in a clean uniform, he poured the coffee into an extra-large travel mug and wolfed down two toasted peanut butter and jelly sandwiches. Comfort food at its finest.

His phone rang as he was swallowing the last bite. It was his chief.

"Morning, boss," he said, grateful that his voice didn't reflect how completely exhausted he was.

"Good morning, Lieutenant. I trust you slept well."

He grimaced. He couldn't lie to the chief of police. "Not particularly, but I'll do."

"I hear you." The chief paused, then filled him in. "Michaela had the early shift today and had to leave. Sergeant Murphy called out this morning. Some kind of stomach bug. He can't go and pick up Katie, and I don't want to take Joe away from his post at Michaela's. We can't leave Leila and Evie unprotected. Are you available to pick her up?"

Now that he thought about it, John Murphy had looked a little pale before he left the station the day before.

"Sure, I can drive out and get Katie, Chief." He wanted to check on Leila, anyway. This would be the perfect excuse.

"Do you remember where her house is?"

"I have a pretty good idea. I can put it in my GPS. I'll be in a little bit later than planned."

"Bring Leila when you come in. For the time being, it's best if she's not on her own."

"She's not going to like that."

"She'll be alive. That's all I care about."

As long as they kept someone with Evie, he was good. And he knew Michaela. That woman was serious about security. Out of respect, he didn't ask about her past, but he'd heard her say enough to know she'd gone into law enforcement after some kind of trauma.

He grabbed his coffee mug and then jogged out to his car. After connecting his phone to the car, he plugged in Katie's address and backed out of the driveway. The sun kept peeking out of the clouds, playing a game of hide-and-seek. He had a feeling the clouds would win. The scent of rain rode heavy in the air.

Twenty minutes into the drive, Brett admitted he had no idea where he was. If he hadn't had his GPS, he never would have found her place. The area was rural, with dirt roads and missing street signs. Even though he'd driven Katie home the night before, it was still hard. He'd had her to direct him then. But looking around, everything looked the same. It would be easy to get hopelessly lost out here. He liked the country, but not this much.

Switching on his turn signal, he pulled up to the house. Before he could exit the vehicle, though, Katie appeared at the door. She must have recognized him, because she waved before holding up one finger. Then she disappeared, only to return a minute later carrying a sturdy tote bag. An older man and woman, most likely her parents, followed her to the door. She waved to them before running down to the car. Brett opened the car door for her, took her tote bag—it weighed a ton—and placed it in the back seat.

Brett hurried back to his side of the cruiser. Leila and Evie had to both be awake by now. The chief or Joe or Michaela would have reached out if they had any concerns. After all, he was the lieutenant heading this case. The fact that he hadn't heard anything was good news.

He glanced at his cell phone to make sure they weren't in a dead zone. He had enough bars.

"*Gut* morning, Brett," Katie greeted him after buckling herself in. "I didn't expect you to pick me up today."

He turned around in the driveway and let the GPS guide him toward Michaela's house. "We had a bit of an incident yesterday."

Calmly, he gave her a toned-down version of what had happened at Leila's house after she left. He didn't want to scare her, but she needed to understand that there was some danger involved with her babysitting duties now.

"Leila and Evie are *gut*? They are unharmed?" The first note of anxiety touched her voice.

"Yes. Both are well. And we will always have police protection on the premises. Plus, Officer Witt has an excellent security system in place."

He risked a glance at Katie. Her expression remained calm, as if he hadn't just explained a murderer was after Leila. Surely she had to be upset. But maybe not. The anxiety he had heard in her voice earlier seemed to have dissipated. Or maybe she was really skilled at masking her feelings. "Are you all right?"

"*Ja.* I'm *gut*."

"Even though I told you—"

"*Gott* will handle it."

He had faith. But Katie's was in a whole other league.

The rain started about two minutes from Michaela's house. His fingers tensed on the steering wheel. He was almost there. His radio remained silent, as had his phone. He told himself everything was fine at Michaela's place. No security alarms had been tripped.

Still, he didn't breathe easily until he swung into the U-shaped driveway and saw Joe's cruiser parked in front of the house. The younger officer met him at the front door.

"Sir, no disturbances overnight. Officer Witt left for work an hour ago."

"Very good, Officer. What is the schedule?"

"I'm here until three. Officer Zilhaver will replace me at that time."

"Sounds good. Don't let your guard down. No mistakes."

"Yes, sir."

Brett motioned for Katie to go ahead of him. He walked behind the young Amish woman, deeper into the house, following the trail of voices and the occasional childish giggle. When they entered the kitchen, Leila and Evie were both sitting in the small breakfast nook. Evie forked a bite of fluffy pancake into her mouth. The scents of pancake syrup and cinnamon swirled in the air.

"Smells mighty tasty in here." Brett inhaled deeply. "Did you eat them all, Evie?"

The little girl giggled. "Yep. They all gone, Brett."

"I can make more—" Leila started to rise.

"Nah. I'm just joshing you. I already ate. Katie's here."

Her gaze darted to her babysitter. When she looked back at Brett, she beamed at him, gratitude in her eyes.

That smile punched its way through all his emotional defenses. He froze.

What had caused that deer-in-the-headlights stare?

Leila's smile faded and she flushed. Had she done something wrong?

"Brett?"

He shook himself out of whatever mood he was in. "Sorry. Something struck me. Are you about ready to head in to the station? I'll give you a lift."

Startled, she straightened in her seat. "Oh, I assumed I'd drive myself over. No need for you to wait for me."

He looked at her funny, as if she'd said something really dumb. "Um, isn't the point that you aren't to be by yourself? I realize that you want to be independent, but what if this guy tails you and catches you when you're unaware?"

She tightened her lips. If there was one thing she hated, it was feeling boxed in. Not having her own vehicle with her, having a shadow 24-7—that was pretty much the definition of being boxed in. They might as well put her in a cage.

She scolded herself for acting like a child. The important thing was finding her sister's killer. Tara's face, white and bloated from the water, danced in front of her. She squeezed her eyes tight. No matter how she felt, she'd cooperate. Brett and Michaela and the rest of the department were going out of their way to keep her and Evie safe from a serial killer. The brief flare of resistance sputtered out, leaving her weary.

Why was she always so belligerent? It never made any sense. On the one hand, she was so sick of always being alone. She didn't have a lot of friends—in fact, there really wasn't anyone that she trusted one hundred percent. And it was all her fault. She tended to push people away. She knew she did.

Ever since Tara died, she hadn't let anyone get too close to her—not even her husband, which was probably why he'd had an affair. Briefly, she wondered if he'd still be alive if she had opened her heart to him like she should have. Would he have still strayed?

None of these questions could ever be answered, of course. She would never know. *Enough stewing over the past*, she told herself. That wasn't going to help her at all.

Abruptly, she stood.

"I just need to go get my umbrella and my purse, and I'll be right with you," she told Brett.

"I'll be out on the front porch. I need to talk with Joe for a minute." He turned to Evie and smiled at her. "I'll see you later, princess."

"I'm not a princess!" Evie giggled again.

He winked. "Sure you are. Bye."

"Bye!" she sang to him.

The little exchange melted Leila's heart—just a little. She bent down and gave her daughter a hug and a kiss.

"Mommy's got to go to work now, sweetie. You mind Katie and don't make any trouble for her. You're going to have to stay in today, because it's going to keep raining."

Evie pushed her bottom lip out in the most adorable pout. "But I don't want to stay inside! I want to go outside and play in the sun! And so does Priscilla!"

Leila laughed. Priscilla was Evie's toy unicorn that she carried with her everywhere. She'd gotten it for her birthday. Leila didn't even know where the name Priscilla came from. It was just so adorable hearing her daughter say it with her cute little lisp.

"Well, darling, I don't think Priscilla wants to get wet. If she gets muddy, we might not be able to clean her."

After a thoughtful glance at the unicorn, Evie nodded sadly.

"Okay," she said. "Priscilla wants to stay clean."

"Yeah, I thought she did," Leila said, ruffling her daughter's hair once more. She loved the feel of her soft curls.

She hurried to the guest room where they had slept and grabbed her raincoat, umbrella and purse. She stopped back in the kitchen to refill her coffee and add another splash of French vanilla creamer when her phone dinged.

It was an all-call sent out from the police department with a picture of the murdered woman. It was one that she'd taken yesterday. Leila only hoped that once all the departments circulated the image, they would find someone who could identify her.

Katie gasped.

Startled, Leila jerked her eyes off her phone. The Amish girl stood at her shoulder, her gaze glued to Leila's phone screen. Oh. She hadn't meant for her to see such a shocking sight. "Sorry. I'll put it away—"

"I know her."

"You what?"

Tears trickled down Katie's bloodless cheeks. "I know her. She's Amish. Or she used to be."

"Brett!" Leila wound an arm around Katie's shoulder and led her to the couch. Katie collapsed on the cushion, crying quietly into her apron. Leila joined her.

Brett hurtled through the door to meet them in the kitchen. "Leila! What's wrong?"

She pointed to Katie. "Victim seven. Katie knew her."

"Hold on a second." Brett pulled out his phone and placed a call. He tapped the speaker icon. A few seconds later, the chief's voice came on the line. "Chief, we're here with Katie, Leila's babysitter. She saw the image of the girl found yesterday and says she knows her."

The chief was silent for only a moment. "Katie, if you can identify her, we'd be grateful."

Katie choked back a sob. "*Ja.* I'm *gut*. Just shocked. Her name is—was—Zillah Miller. Her family was in the district next to mine. We saw each other at singings and events. When she was sixteen or so, her *daed* argued with the bishop and the whole family was shunned. They left and became Mennonite. I haven't seen her in four years. Maybe a little more."

Brett hunkered in front of her. "Katie, how are you sure

it's her? You haven't seen her in so long, and people change so much at that age."

Katie swiped the back of her hand across her wet cheeks. "*Nee*, not that much. She looks almost exactly like her cousin Margaret, who is still in the next district."

"We'll have to bring in her parents to identify the body," Chief Kaiser said. "I'm sorry, Katie, but do you know their address?"

She didn't, but she had their names, so the chief looked them up. "I'll send Michaela to pick them up. Leila, I just had an idea. I find it unlikely that TBK would know of the victim's connection to Katie. After all, she wasn't part of the same community when she died, and you and Katie didn't know each other until you moved back. However, I do think that we should keep Katie and Evie here at the station instead of at Michaela's. I need all my officers working on this. If Katie stays here, we can protect you and your daughter better while she watches the child."

Leila wrinkled her brow, thinking. "I hear what you're saying. I'm not sure if a police station is the best place for an active four-year-old, though."

The chief was undeterred. "Let's be cautious. Brett, bring them in today. Then we can make plans."

She wasn't about to argue with the chief.

"I'll go." Katie stood. "I will see Zillah's family."

"Will you be allowed to talk with them?" Leila asked.

"Maybe not, but I hope it will comfort them to have someone who knew the family there."

Leila packed up her daughter and a few toys to keep her busy. They piled into Brett's cruiser. Joe agreed to follow them to the station. This case was becoming stranger every minute.

* * *

Brett hated coincidences. They made everything a tangled mess. Now he needed to figure out if Katie was in danger because of her relationship with Leila, or if Leila was correct and TBK had targeted Zillah Miller because she matched the approximate height, build, hair color and skin tone of his previous victims. The more he thought about it, the more Leila seemed to be on to the truth. How many people expected a Mennonite woman to go jogging? It seemed unreal that Katie had recognized her after so many years.

Like he said. Messy.

Once they arrived at the station, Joe quickly took charge of Evie. He had a way with kids. Evie warmed up to him in no time and soon he had claimed the bag of Play-Doh, toys, crayons and coloring books. He held out a hand to Evie, and within minutes he and the little girl had taken over the smaller conference room.

Brett obtained Joe's promise to text if anything went wrong before joining the chief, Leila and Katie.

A tense forty-five minutes later, Edna and Harrison Miller entered the room, pale and shaken but with a hint of hope in their eyes.

They're hoping we have the wrong girl.

The moment they saw Katie, that hope vanished. Edna gasped Katie's name, then began weeping loudly. Harrison clenched his jaw, blinking rapidly.

They knew.

Katie approached the older woman and reached for her hands, although she didn't say a word. The older woman clung to the young Amish woman's hands for a moment before nodding and dropping them.

"Why doesn't she hug her?" Brett breathed close to Leila's ear, his voice pitched too soft for anyone else to hear.

The scent of vanilla drifting off her skin distracted him. He backed away.

"They were shunned. Even holding her hand is more than they usually do, but these are unusual circumstances."

The small group went together to the morgue located on the next floor up to see the body. Although Brett and Leila had walked with the family, they waited outside of the room to give them some degree of privacy, although they could still view what was happening through the one-way window in the corridor between the morgue and the department.

"I wish I could help them." Leila paced in front of the window, hugging herself. "I remember my parents going to identify Tara. It was horrible."

Brett leaned against the wall. "Yeah. I didn't have to identify my mom, but I was there when she died. It's never pretty."

Her gaze shot to his. "I'm so sorry, Brett."

Why had he said that? He never talked about his mom's death. "It happened a long time ago."

Not so long ago that he'd forgotten the smell of the room, a bottle of his dad's preferred alcohol in pieces on the floor. The fury and fear racing through his body. He'd been eighteen, too old to be taken into foster care. He still wasn't sure if that was a blessing or a curse. He'd had to make it on his own. Thankfully, Carter had been there, like always, to help him through. He didn't even want to think of what he'd have done without his best friend to lean on.

His attention returned to the scene playing out behind the glass. The parents swayed and clung to each other when they saw their daughter's face. He didn't need to hear the conversation to know they'd positively identified her.

The chief returned to the room when the family had gone. "I had Michaela bring the Millers home. Katie insisted that she stay with Evie. She's next door. Leila, you should plan on working out of this office for now. That way, if you are to be sent to a crime scene, I can make sure you have a police escort."

Leila nodded. "I guess that makes sense. I'll be safer here."

She didn't sound too sure of that.

"Do you need anything from your lab?"

She tilted her head, considering. "Yeah, I should stop by there and gather some equipment."

Brett pushed himself away from the wall. "I'll give you a lift. If we don't dawdle, we can be back here in an hour."

"Are you sure? I don't want to keep you away from your duties."

"Well, until we catch this guy, you are part of my duties."

Her head ducked. From where he stood, he saw a tide of red flow up her face before it disappeared beneath her hair. A groan left him. "I didn't mean it that way. Honest. Just know I take your safety seriously."

She nodded without meeting his gaze. "Of course. I understand."

Chief Kaiser glared at him.

Brett puffed his cheeks out and let the air escape in a stream. He couldn't win today. Giving up, he moved to the door.

"You ready?" he asked.

"As ready as I'm going to be," she replied.

She stopped by the conference room and informed Katie and her daughter of the plan before joining him at the front of the station.

As he drove toward the main crime lab situated in Erie, Leila sat quietly. He racked his brain for something he could say to defuse the tension caused by his poor choice of words. Before he could say anything, she shifted in her seat to face him.

"I do want to thank you for giving me a ride today. I know that being on babysitter duty is probably not what you wanted to do with your day." Her laugh sounded false. Yep, he'd definitely hurt her feelings.

"Hey, I don't mind. Really. Like the chief said, you're one of us now. I'd do this for any of the others, you know."

Her brow puckered in a cute little frown. The temptation to smooth the ridges on her forehead shocked him. Since when did he think about things like that? Clearing his throat, he looked forward.

"You all right? You're frowning." He glanced at the rearview mirror.

Her eyes jerked to his face again.

"Sorry. Just thinking about this case. I find it hard to believe that all this is happening because some guy I don't remember is obsessed with me. There has to be another motive. I know I was supposed to be his first victim. But why? Did I remind him of someone? And why did he stop killing? And then start again?"

He frowned and filed through all the facts they had up to this point. "I've been thinking about that. He didn't come after you in Colorado. So why now?"

"Good question. I was gone for nearly five years. Maybe once I got married, I fell off the radar?"

"Maybe. But it's not like a good internet search wouldn't find your wedding information, along with your married name."

"True. And I returned almost two years ago. So why now?"

Leila leaned her head against the cool window and pondered his words.

"I wonder—" she finally mused aloud. "We kept our marriage very quiet. No big ceremony or reception. My mother was gone—she'd died four years after Tara's murder. My dad had pretty much checked out of my life, out of everything. Will—my husband—was an only child who didn't really get along with his folks. So we had a very small event. I never sent a notice to the papers. If he knew me, he could have specifically searched for marriages by my name. That's if he knew me. Plus," she added as she sat up, "most people spell my name L-a-y-l-a. If he was someone who knew of me but didn't know me well, he might have searched for me by that spelling. I looked it up last night after our conversation. I found at least ten other women by that name."

Brett reached for his travel mug at the same time she put her hand on hers. Their hands collided. She couldn't ignore the zing that pulsed up her arm. She grabbed her coffee and tried to pretend nothing out of the ordinary had happened. When she peeked at him out of the corner of her eye, he calmly sipped his own drink, as if he'd felt nothing.

Annoyed, she gulped a large mouthful, nearly scalding her mouth in the process. It wasn't fair that he could be so unaffected by her presence.

She didn't have time for men in her life. What did it matter if he was attractive? Or if he made her feel safe? All of it was a lie. Only she could protect herself.

Not even God had protected her family ten years ago.

Sometimes, she missed the days when she'd go into church and feel awed, like she could sense His presence. But it wasn't real. Because Tara and her mom were both gone, her dad had abandoned her and remarried, and her husband had died in the arms of another woman. All she had was her precious little girl.

That was all she needed.

Once they arrived at the forensics lab, she opened her

door. “I’ll only be a few minutes. I need to explain the situation to my boss and then gather anything I might need over the next couple of days. I’m off for two days after that.”

“No problem. I’ll come with.”

It seemed a bit overkill to her. After all, she was within feet of the door, and his car was right there. But she shrugged and went along with it. After all, she was “part of his duties.” Then shame filled her. He’d felt bad about his phrasing—she’d seen that. Why did she hold it against him? Sometimes she didn’t like how cynical she’d become since her sister’s death. *I need to do better.*

Letting things go had been easier before her faith had been shattered. For a second, she had the urge to pray. Strange. She hadn’t voluntarily talked to God for years, and now she’d thought of reaching out to God twice in two days.

She led the way to her boss’s office. When she knocked, Dean waved her in. “Leila. I just got off the phone with Chief Kaiser. How are you holding up?”

“As well as can be expected,” she assured him. “I just came to get my equipment so I can continue working.”

He eyed her critically. “If you need time, you let me know.”

“I will. Hopefully, I won’t.”

“I’ll have Shane help you carry your stuff.”

“It won’t be necessary. I have help.” She jerked a thumb over her shoulder at Brett.

“I see that. But you might need more than one person.”

She wasn’t in the habit of arguing with her boss, so she gave in gracefully with a casual one-shoulder shrug.

“Follow me,” she beckoned Brett. A minute later, she opened the door to her office and made a face. Unlike her house, which was neat and ultra-organized, chaos reigned supreme in this space. It wasn’t that it was messy—it was just that she had such a small area to keep large amounts of equipment—various cameras, tripods, lenses, lights and cords.

"Wow." Brett stood in the middle of the room and slowly rotated in a full circle. "This is impressive."

When he said it that way, it didn't sound like a compliment.

Leila chuckled, trying to see it through his eyes. "I do have quite the collection, don't I? Well, thankfully, we won't have to carry all of it. I just want to make sure that if we get called to a scene, I have what I need. The weather is supposed to be rainy the next few days, so I'll need a little bit more than normal."

As quickly as she could manage without risking breaking anything, she gathered what she needed, stuffing the items carefully into various bags. She zipped the last bag as someone knocked on the door.

Peering at the entrance, she waved for Shane, one of the maintenance men, to enter.

"Leila. The boss said you needed me to carry some equipment."

"Yeah." She glanced around at her bags. "I think this will work. Between the three of us, we can get everything in one trip."

They did—barely. Shane and Brett handled the larger bags. They stuffed some of the equipment in the trunk, and the rest in the back of the cruiser.

"I hope I don't have to arrest anyone on the drive back to Sterling Ridge," Brett muttered. "We might have to put them on top of the cruiser."

She elbowed him. "Thanks, Shane. I appreciate your help."

After he'd disappeared inside the building, she and Brett

got back into the cruiser and headed back to Sterling Ridge. She wanted to see Evie. Even knowing her daughter was in a safe place, this case had her unsettled. The knot in her stomach felt like it was made of cement.

The radio crackled to life. The dispatcher's voice echoed inside the car.

"All units. Body discovered on Pier Four. Coroner is en route."

The invisible knot in her gut became a fist, clenching her insides painfully.

Brett responded. "I'm on the way. The forensic photographer is with me."

He flipped on his lights and siren and did a U-turn at the intersection. The early-morning traffic pulled to the side of the street and allowed him to speed past. His jaw looked like it had been chiseled from stone. Anger and purpose emanated from him.

She swallowed. Was this body another victim of TBK? Maybe number eight?

Leila clenched her trembling hands together in her lap. She didn't buy that this was a coincidence. Two bodies washed up two days in a row? No, in her gut she knew this was somehow related to the Brand Killer.

Every silent mile they drove brought them one step closer to the evil committed by a serial killer.

One who had marked her as his prey.

SEVEN

Rain pelted the windshield. Water streamed down the glass, cutting visibility to a mere foot. Brett increased the wiper speed to full blast, sending them swishing across the surface every second. The steering wheel shuddered. The pavement was too slick for the cruiser to handle the current speed. As much as he deplored the loss of time, he slowed his vehicle. It wouldn't help anyone if he hydroplaned and wrecked.

The woman beside him sat still, like she'd become a statue. Concerned, he shot a quick side glance in her direction. Her lovely face was taut and slightly pale. But those eyes stared out the window with a piercing glare.

She didn't look scared or worried.

She looked like a Valkyrie, a warrior ready for a fight.

"There!" She pointed to the right side of the road. Through the onslaught of rain, blurry red and blue lights flashed at them. "That's got to be at least four cruisers."

"Hmm. Three cruisers and the coroner's car," he corrected.

Brett parked behind Deanna's vehicle. He'd recognize it anywhere; it resembled an old-fashioned hearse. She stepped out of her vehicle when she saw them.

"Leila. Brett." Deanna gave them a single nod, then opened her umbrella. "I just arrived myself."

Leila grabbed her camera from the back seat of Brett's cruiser. He hurried over to her with an umbrella. "Hold on."

He watched her duck back in and pull something large and awkward from a bag. It took him a moment to realize she was grabbing a tripod.

"Why a tripod?"

"Because it's raining. I need to have the camera far enough away to control the flash. Every drop of rain will create a glare, which could mess up the images. Trust me, this weather can really make collecting digital evidence tricky, but it can be done. You guys are going to have to be a little more patient than usual, though. It's going to take a little longer."

Securing the area with crime-scene tape, Brian Roberts groaned when she said that.

"Do you have a complaint, Sergeant?" Brett snapped. He wasn't angry, but he expected a certain level of decorum at a crime scene.

Brian straightened sharply. "No, sir. No complaints."

Brett sighed. "Easy, Brian. Look, I know this is hard, standing in the rain at a crime scene. I get it. But we have to do the hard work to get justice for whoever they pulled from the water. There's a process for that. And we have to follow it to the letter. You know what I'm saying?"

"I know. Sorry for my impatience. I just don't like the rain."

"Most people don't. But this is your job."

Leila stepped to his side. "Are you coming with me?"

He motioned for her to lead the way. When she got to the crime-scene tape, he lifted it for her to cross to the other side. "I'll wait for you here."

He would make sure nothing got to her.

She approached the body. He had a visceral reaction, an urge to swoop in and pull her out. Even from where he stood, the level of decomposition appalled him. This woman had been in the water for months. Possibly even a year. A hunk of dark hair clung to the back of the skull, and only some material remained from her clothing.

It made his stomach churn. He'd been a cop too long to become squeamish at the sight of a body. Still, there were some things that no human should ever see or suffer through.

Deep in his bones, he believed they'd found the missing sixth TBK victim.

Get a grip, Brett. You're here to protect Leila.

He recalled his words to Brian earlier. Those same words applied to him now. He had a job to do. And this young woman deserved justice.

He crossed his arms and surveyed the area, squinting his eyes to see better through the rain. Watching Leila work fascinated him. Her intensity and the precision with which she set up her equipment and took each shot impressed him. She didn't just get images of the body, either. She worked on documenting the entire scene.

It had to bother her, getting so close to another murder victim. Even a body so badly decomposed. Clearly, this woman had died in a similar way to her own sister. Yet, her professional mask never slipped. Picture after picture she snapped. Every few pictures, she'd move the tripod.

"I have one more angle, then I'll be done," she called to him.

He gave her a thumbs-up. The team would be happy that they could come in and process the scene.

"Brett!" she shrieked, stumbling back from the body.

Brett hurtled over the crime-scene tape and raced to her side. The rest of the officers swarmed in around the tape. They didn't cross over, but they were ready to jump into action at his order.

Leila pointed at the face. While the features were no longer clear, the duct tape across the mouth appeared fresh. As if it had been placed there recently.

This body, like the one the day before, had the wrists and ankles taped together. The bindings appeared to have suffered the same wear as the victim had.

"There are drag marks." Brett pointed to them. "Recent. I would say the killer wanted this body found here."

Apparently, the killer was tired of waiting for them to find the body. The evil of the person who did this made him sick.

"It's TBK," she whispered.

He placed a cautious hand on her shoulder. He didn't want to appear too forward, but neither could he stand by and not offer comfort like he would any other person.

"I think you're right, although I don't see a brand."

"Not anymore, but look at the mouth."

The duct tape. Lime green. Written on the tape, he saw the large, black number six. It wasn't that that made cold fingers crawl up his spine. It was the message under the number.

SHOULD HAVE BEEN LAYLA

He'd spelled her name wrong. So maybe it was a stalker. But why had he fixated on Leila?

He saw the agony on her face.

"None of this is your fault, Leila. You didn't encourage this or in any way cause him to do these horrible things."

"I know." Her voice was a thin, hollow sound. "Mentally, I know. But I don't think I'll have any peace of mind until he's caught."

"We'll catch him." He shouldn't promise such things; there was no way he could be sure they would catch TBK. The killer had been free to create mayhem for ten years. Deep in his soul, Brett knew he wouldn't rest easily until Leila and Evie were out of harm's way. The only way to do that for good was to put this animal in a cage and throw away the key.

Leila could barely breathe through the emotions crushing her chest. Fear, anger, pain, sorrow, guilt—they were all in there, layered one on top of another. Who was this guy? Why had he settled on her for his obsession?

He couldn't have known her well. Not with how he spelled her name. Or that he hadn't realized she'd had a twin. Everyone who knew her growing up knew about Tara. In high school, they hadn't been called Tara and Leila. Their friends—even the staff—at Sterling Ridge High School referred to them as "the twins."

She'd hear people say, "I'm taking one of the twins to the dance." Like it didn't matter which one. Or "I have one the twins in my biology lab."

Their mom had thought having identical girls was so fun and had always dressed them alike as children. But when they morphed into rebellious teens, they never wore the same clothes on the same day, even though they shared a closet and swapped clothes all the time.

No, this killer hadn't known her at all.

A hand on her elbow made her jump.

"Sorry," Deanna murmured. "I need to get in here if you're done."

She read her friend's concern and tried to smile to reassure her. Her lips trembled. "I've gotten all I need."

"If you want to return to my cruiser, I'll escort you." Brett appeared at her side. Leila grimaced. She understood the need for an escort. If she'd had her own vehicle, though, she could have taken her camera and work tools and headed to the station rather than hanging around until he finished. Her presence held him back from completing his duty efficiently.

It wasn't her fault, she reminded herself. Brett hovered at her elbow, waiting for her reply.

"I can get to the car without an escort."

"I'm sure you can," he said as he touched her arm gently. "But I'm here."

He wouldn't say that he was her personal guard, but she understood his meaning.

"Fine."

He slanted his concerned glance at her, letting her know he wasn't fooled. She was anything but fine. Her soul was spiraling. Control was a lie. She had no control over any of this.

She cast one last look down at the body on the ground. A sob welled up inside. She quelled it before it could break free. Somewhere, a family was waiting to hear what had happened to their daughter.

"I want to know when she's identified."

"You will," Brett promised. Neither of them voiced the horrid possibility that she might never be identified. If she hadn't been reported missing, or if her DNA wasn't on file, she might end up being just another Jane Doe. If that happened, Dee would have her cremated and the ashes stored at the morgue.

He placed a hand on her elbow. They began to head toward the vehicle.

"Lieutenant Talbot!"

At the sound of his name, Brett stopped. She could see the agony of indecision on his face as he weighed leaving her on her own or going where he was called.

"Ryan!" he barked.

Sergeant Douglass trotted over. "Sir?"

"Please escort Leila to my cruiser. Do not leave her."

"Yes, sir."

Brett wheeled away and headed to the officer who'd called his name. Ryan gestured for her to go ahead of him. She cast one last look behind her at Brett, now standing in a group of law enforcement in a serious conversation.

They walked silently past the first two police vehicles, lights still flashing, when she remembered all the very expensive equipment she'd carelessly walked away from.

"Oh!" She spun in the opposite direction. "I forgot my camera and tripod."

Her face burned. What kind of photographer left that kind of equipment out in the rain?

One that had just seen something beyond horrific. She couldn't deny it. The memory of victim six would haunt her for a long time, possibly for the remainder of her life. Someday, she promised herself, she'd get out of this field and turn to photographing weddings and retirement parties. Maybe even horse events at the local fairs.

No more bodies and crime scenes.

She started speed walking back to the crime scene.

"Wait! Leila, wait up."

She glanced over her shoulder to see Ryan striding in her direction.

Crack!

Ryan flew off his feet and crashed to the ground. A dark stain bloomed across the shoulder of his gray uniform. Shouts echoed around her.

Leila forgot about her camera and tripod and rushed toward Ryan, who lay groaning on the wet grass, clutching his bloody shoulder. She could see red seeping between his fingers.

She passed the second cruiser. Before she reached Ryan, long arms snagged her and covered her mouth. Then she was pulled, kicking and trying to scream, away from the scene. Her cries were muffled against her assailant's gloved hands. She tried to bite him, but her teeth couldn't cut through the material. Her captor dragged her into the brush and across the rocks.

Despite all the precautions they had taken, even with the presence of multiple police officers, the killer had found her. She was going to die the same way her sister had.

She prayed, desperately.

God, if You're there, help me!

Had she waited too long to reach out to Him?

EIGHT

The single gunshot halted all conversation.

Leila!

Brett whipped away from Deanna and removed his Glock from its holster. He kept it pointed at the ground, ready to fire at a moment's notice. Where was Ryan? Had he fired his gun? Instinctively, Brett knew he hadn't. With so many law enforcement officers in the vicinity, Ryan would have called for backup if there were concerns. And if he had taken care of a problem, he would have reported in.

Ryan Douglass always followed protocol.

"Michaela! Brian! With me." Brett charged in the direction of his cruiser. He called out orders to the others working around the crime scene to protect its integrity and keep their eyes open for another attack.

His hard-soled shoes sank into the wet ground, slowing his progress. The rain continued to beat down on them as he and his officers raced toward the last place they had seen Ryan and Leila. Through the thick curtain of droplets, he saw a body crumpled on the ground.

"Ryan!" Brett dropped to his knees beside his colleague, unconcerned with the mud seeping into his uniform pants.

Ryan groaned, eyes squeezed shut.

Brett ripped his uniform shirt open. Buttons flew in every

direction. He tore off the shirt, leaving his black T-shirt in place, and handed it to Brian. "Here. Use this. Press down on the wound and try to stem the bleeding. Michaela, contact the chief. We need an ambulance and more backup, if any are available. I'm going after Leila."

Brian grabbed the shirt and replaced Brett at Ryan's side. He wadded the cloth into a thick square and pushed Ryan's hands away. When he placed the shirt on the bloody wound, the lieutenant groaned.

He was alive. For now.

Michaela had the chief on the phone. "Lieutenant Douglass is down, shot by an unknown assailant. Leila is missing. We need—"

Brett didn't stay to hear the rest. They had it under control, as much as they could. An ambulance was on the way. His goal was to make sure Deanna Snow didn't have another body to work on. The idea he might find Leila dead chilled him to the soul. He pushed himself faster.

There were new tracks in the ground. Two sets of prints. The larger footprints were clear. The small set sometimes appeared stretched out, as if the person were being dragged. Every few steps, the marks were jumbled up.

She's alive. Alive and fighting him.

A small glimmer of hope settled in his mind. If her captor hadn't killed her yet, Brett had a chance. Maybe the assailant didn't want to kill her outright but preferred to remove her from the scene so that he could take his time, possibly to deal with her the same way as he had the other victims.

The acid in his gut churned as Brett continued to stalk his prey. Finding victim number six had not been by chance. It had been a deliberate setup. A gruesome plan to get Leila out in the open. Now that it was evident Leila was the forensic photographer on the case, the victim's body had been taken from wherever her final resting place had been and staged on the shore as bait.

They had had no choice but to respond. What disturbed him most was the chilling accuracy with which the killer had almost mortally wounded an officer, matched with the willingness—the audacity—to set off these events when it had to be expected that Leila wouldn't be alone. Or undefended. His ability to fire at Ryan and snatch Leila indicated serious skills. And planning.

Brett discarded the idea the killer had aimed for Leila. No, he had already proven that he had other plans for her. According to her statement from the previous day, he'd tried to pull her out the window with him and had only resorted to trying to strangle her when it became clear he wouldn't be able to escape with her. No, he'd deliberately shot Ryan to nab her. To do so in an area crawling with law enforcement meant he was either highly confident in his own skills, or desperate, or his obsession with Leila had completely driven him off the deep end and he was willing to take any risk to finish his deadly quest.

Brett stopped. The muddy ground gave way to a luscious layer of green grass. He peered closer to find the direction they had gone. There! Three feet up and to the left a clump of grass had been uprooted viciously. Most likely by Leila's boots. He turned in that direction.

What was that?

Brett halted, holding his breath. There it was again. Somewhere in the trees, he heard a disturbance. To his trained ears, it sounded like a struggle. And an engine.

The killer had dragged Leila to his getaway car.

Adrenaline flooded Brett's system. He forced himself to remain calm and be cautious. If he burst through the tree line, he'd alert the killer. And maybe get himself or Leila killed in the process.

Checking his hold on his weapon, Brett advanced. In the distance, the wail of sirens pierced the air. Good. The ambulance had arrived. A second later, his satisfaction dissipated, replaced by a new urgency.

Soon, the beach and tree line would be full of officers searching for Leila and her captor. Which might push the killer past all caution. He'd resorted to trying to strangle her before. This time, however, Brett knew the man possessed a gun. At close range, he wouldn't miss.

Brett needed to get to them first.

Pushing himself faster, he approached the tree line. A woman cried out, pain and fury vibrating in her voice. Brett's heart pounded.

"No! I won't go!"

He burst through the trees. Before him, Leila wrestled with a man in a leather jacket. He wore a gruesome Grim Reaper mask and gloves. It was the same man he'd seen the night before. They stood next to a van with its door open. He was trying to force her into the vehicle, but her feet kicked at it, pushing herself away from the van.

"Let her go!" Brett raised his Glock. The attacker whirled to face him, Leila tight against his chest. He didn't dare flick the safety off. Not until he had a clear shot. He couldn't risk pulling the trigger with Leila there. He moved sideways, trying for a better angle. Brett took no pleasure in shooting anyone. Death was final. It should never be taken lightly.

But he would kill to protect the innocent. If he had to.

He desperately hoped the killer would make a better choice.

Leila's breath escaped in raspy pants. Brett had arrived. She read the frustration in his scowl. She was in his way.

Her captor chuckled in her ear. "He can't shoot me. Not unless he wants you dead, too."

She renewed her struggles.

"I'll kill him, too, princess. See if I don't." He tightened his right arm around her, ignoring her kicks and twists. Then he raised the semiautomatic gun, the one that had shot Ryan, and flicked off the safety. "Say goodbye."

"Brett!" she screamed.

The gun fired near her ear.

Brett dodged out of the way. The bullet buried itself in a tree trunk a foot behind where he'd stood seconds ago. As the two men circled, Leila recalled how she'd gotten away the day before. But this time she couldn't fall forward. The position of his body and the way he had her imprisoned against him had her feet almost dangling. Only the balls of her feet and her toes were on the ground.

When he shifted, her left foot landed flat on the ground. It was like a tripod. Holding her breath, she yanked her feet completely off the ground. For a second they teetered before tipping over.

The arm pinning her to the killer dropped away. Leila crashed on the dirt and rolled away from him. He caught himself and his fingers clawed at her. When she evaded his grasp, he cursed and raised his gun.

Brett had taken advantage of the villain's distraction and bridged the gap until he stood ten feet from them. The killer's finger tightened on the trigger. Before he could complete the shot, Brett fired his weapon. With a scream, the killer dropped the gun. Blood dripped from the palm of his gloved hand to the ground. Swearing again, the attacker threw himself into the driver's seat of the van.

Brett ran the last ten feet toward her. Once he was at her

side, he shot at the van. The bullet dinged the rear taillight. Then the van rounded a sharp curve and roared out of sight.

"I'm sorry." Brett hunched at her side, his searing gaze meeting hers before he scanned her. "I couldn't shoot at the van when you were so close to it. A bullet could have ricocheted off it and struck you. Are you okay? I don't see any injuries."

She shook her head. Suddenly, the impact of what had almost happened overwhelmed her. Bursting into tears, Leila threw her arms around Brett's neck and sobbed into his shoulder.

He wobbled a bit. It had to be uncomfortable crouching down, balancing like that. She should let go. But she couldn't. When his arms lifted her slightly, she didn't realize what was happening until he shifted and sat on the ground, settling her on his lap. His strong arms rocked her while the tears continued to pour from her eyes. Slowly, she calmed down. Her sobs dwindled to a few sniffles.

"Easy. You're safe, Leila."

She realized while she'd cried, he'd been talking. A soothing stream of comforting words. She nearly smiled; it reminded her of how she talked to Evie when her daughter was frightened.

Leila pulled away from him. "If you weren't already soaked from the rain, you would be now. I'm sorry. I don't know what happened."

Brett lowered his head a little to gaze directly into her eyes. The intensity of the look startled her. "I think you've been through a very traumatic two days."

Leila heard a noise and jerked her head to the right. Embarrassed, she realized they were surrounded by a paramedic and three officers. She flushed.

"I'm good." She scrambled to her feet. "Sorry. Didn't mean to embarrass you."

His mouth flattened and his brows crunched down to give her a look that clearly said, *oh please*. "Why would I, or you, need to be embarrassed? Leila, you've seen two bodies that are both connected to your sister's murder. Someone broke into your house and tried to strangle you. And now you were nearly kidnapped. If you hadn't shown some kind of emotional outburst, I'd have wondered if you were even human."

"That's the truth." Michaela trotted to her side and gave her a small side hug before stepping away and facing Brett. "Sir, Lieutenant Douglass in on the way to the hospital. He was awake and coherent when they loaded him in the ambulance."

"And cranky," the paramedic added.

Brett huffed a laugh. After the emotions of the morning she found the sound comforting. "Doesn't surprise me." Relief colored his tone.

"I'd like to check you out, miss," the paramedic informed her.

"I'm fine." She stepped back and her ankle protested. "Ow."

Brett rolled his eyes. "Yeah, you sound like you feel fine."

Leila glared at him. "I'm tired, wet, it's pouring rain. My ankle hurts when I step on it wrong—I had been dragged, as you said—but I can walk without issue. I don't hurt anywhere else, I'm not bleeding and I want to see my daughter."

She clamped her mouth shut when she realized she'd been almost shouting. She tried to pull her dignity back together. "My apologies. I don't mean to yell. But I want to go back to the station."

"Ma'am, if you're refusing treatment, I can't force you. Sign this form and I'll leave you alone." She did so and the paramedic departed.

Michaela stayed with her while the others finished up at the scene. When Brett approached the vehicle, the perky officer patted her shoulder. "Let me know if I can do anything for you."

"I will. I appreciate everything."

When Michaela sauntered away, Leila watched her leave, feeling the emptiness of her life. Brett opened up the trunk of the car. She could hear him riffling around for something.

"You look sad," Brett said.

She startled. She hadn't noticed him shutting the trunk. He had a clean uniform shirt on. "Do I? I guess I am. I just realized that when Michaela talks to me, it's like we're friends."

"And that's bad?"

"It's not bad. It's unusual." She shivered. Her teeth chattered, making it hard to talk.

"You're freezing!" Brett held open the door and encouraged her to get into his vehicle. He ran around to the driver's side and jumped in.

"Don't worry about me. I'll warm up." The clicking of her teeth told a different story.

Brett ignored her statement.

"I should have started the car and turned on the heat. Hold on." A second later, the engine purred to life. "It will take a few minutes for the heat to kick on. We have heated seats. And..." He jumped out and ran to the back. The hatch lifted and then abruptly slammed shut. Brett brought her a blanket. "This should help you warm up faster."

Gratefully, she accepted the blanket. Five minutes later, the heated seats and the blanket had worked their magic. Her teeth stopped chattering. "Oh, that feels nice. I don't remember ever being that cold."

"I'm glad." He turned the heat dial. Warm air pumped

through the vents. "So, why is it unusual? Michaela talking to you like a friend?"

She shifted to see him better. She'd been alone for so long. Confiding in anyone wasn't something she did. But suddenly, the need to tell Brett rose like a wave in her chest. "After Tara died, my entire life changed. We were badgered by reporters. Nothing that sensational had happened in this town for a long time. It had started to die down, then the next victim was found. They decided to revisit Tara's case."

The warmth became a little too much. She shoved the top of the blanket down and tucked it under her arms.

Brett didn't interrupt, so she kept going.

"I took classes. I already had my photography degree. But I needed some forensic courses. I didn't feel like going to college, but I needed to get out of the house. And I wanted to do something that mattered. My mother's every thought was about Tara. It was almost like she'd forgotten she had two daughters. When I decided to pursue forensic photography, both my parents were against it. Hadn't I seen enough of that kind of thing? Why put myself through more? But I needed to feel like I was doing something to stop those who hurt people. That's around the time I met William."

She stopped. Life hadn't gotten any easier.

"Then what happened?"

She brushed a curl off the side of her face. "My mom got cancer. We barely knew she had it and she was gone. It seemed like overnight, my dad moved on. He started going back to church, met someone and married again. I haven't talked to him in two years. It felt like he abandoned me and Evie."

Brett sat still, his posture casual, but she sensed hesitation. A moment later, he spoke. "Why were you alone? What happened with your husband?"

It was too late to decide to stop. But the last part made

her feel icky. "He fell asleep in someone's apartment and died from carbon monoxide poisoning."

His eyes slid over her face. "Someone's apartment?"

She knew he'd catch that. "Yeah. His girlfriend. While his wife and baby were at home, thinking he was on a business trip."

"Idiot."

She nodded, agreeing with the sentiment. "I haven't had much success with friends or relationships. So I don't have any. Except Dee. She wouldn't let me push her away."

Days like today proved why. She had been so sure she needed to continue working. That desire had been replaced with a need to survive. The killer had already proven that he could lure her out. She needed to protect herself and her daughter.

The memory of Brett nearly getting shot and Ryan falling with a shoulder soaked with blood filled her with another worry. How many would die before the Brand Killer was caught?

Brett drove to the Sterling Ridge Police Department, fuming. What kind of man cheated on his wife? He knew it happened. Had seen it with his own father. And he'd promised God that he would rise above his father's example, even when those around him sneered and told him he'd never succeed, that he came from bad stock.

He had succeeded. He'd even gone to college on a wrestling scholarship. Sure, he'd damaged his knee, but he'd made something of his life.

You're still alone.

Brett ignored the nagging voice in his head. He was alone by choice. No one needed a husband scarred by memories that haunted him, brought on by his own dysfunctional family. Heat that had nothing to do with the car's ventilation system rushed through his body. He realized he was grinding his teeth and deliberately opened his mouth. Anger wouldn't help anyone. What was done couldn't be changed.

He prayed for calm and the wisdom needed to solve this case, find a killer and protect Leila and Evie.

At the station, Leila checked on Evie, then began uploading her pictures. She stopped when the chief called her and Brett to meet her in the conference room. They entered the room and joined her at the table.

"I don't know what to do," Chief Kaiser admitted. "We need to focus on this case, but Leila, your presence is actually interfering." She held up a hand when Leila opened her mouth to speak. "It's not your fault. But I think we need to consider moving you and Evie to a safe place for a while."

"Where could they go?" Brett agreed with the theory, but he didn't like the idea of letting them go off without him being there to protect them. "We don't have any safe houses. We're a pretty small department. Are you going to call in the FBI?"

She could, since they were dealing with a serial killer.

"I will call in help. But as to the other, I don't know where to send them."

"They can *cumme* stay with my family."

They all whipped around to see Katie silhouetted in the doorway. They must have left the door open unintentionally.

"That's very sweet," the chief began, "but—"

"Wait." Brett sat straighter. "The idea has merit."

If Leila went off the grid and they could disguise her, wouldn't she be harder to find? They needed to hide her deep in Amish country, though. So deep that, without an address, there would be no way to find her.

NINE

Leila blinked slowly, her mind blank.

"Wait. What? No!" She was done putting others in harm's way. "Katie, how can I do that? It wouldn't be safe for your family."

Katie's jaw jutted forward. "*Gott* will protect us. It is right for us to help you and the *kind*."

"Leila," Brett said slowly, "I won't pretend her offer isn't without risk. But it's not a bad plan, actually."

"How is it not? He found my house. He knows I'm back. Why wouldn't he know that she's my babysitter?"

"She has a point," Chief Kaiser admitted.

"He might know I'm your babysitter. But he doesn't know my family. I have cousins who live near New Wilmington. We can go there."

"We?"

Katie smiled with the corners of her lips tucked in, exposing her dimples. "*Ja.* I could tell my *mamm* and *daed* that I'm going to visit my cousin Vera for a few days. They won't mind. Vera lives almost two hours from here, so it's not likely you'd be found there."

The room was silent for a full minute while the chief thought about the idea. Leila continued to think it was a horrible idea. Brett stood and paced the length of the room.

The intense energy emanating from him made the space seem smaller than it was.

Finally, the chief gave a decisive nod. "It's the best plan we have. I'll have Sergeant Murphy escort you there—"

"Chief," Brett interrupted her. Leila shot him an incredulous look. Did he just cut off his boss?

"Lieutenant Talbot? Do you have something to add?"

Although her inflection didn't show any irritation, Leila got the sense she was astonished by his actions. He'd interrupted her twice!

Brett's ears turned red. He stood and clasped his hands behind his back. "Sorry, Chief. I didn't mean to butt in. Except, well, I was wondering if it would be better for me to continue with Leila and Evie, since I was on the case from the beginning."

If it were up to Leila, he'd be the one with them. But she didn't say anything. It wouldn't do to show preference for one cop over another. She had to work with them all.

Chief Kaiser smiled with a hint of steel. "I do see your point, Lieutenant Talbot. However, given the situation, I want you to remain here. We have an active serial killer, we have one body still unidentified, and as long as Leila is out of sight, I believe that we should be on the watch for more possible victims."

Leila raised her hand, then jerked it down, feeling like a high school kid.

The chief's smile widened. "I saw that hand. Yes, Leila. What's your question?"

"Um, TBK didn't move that fast before. Why do you expect him to do so now?"

The chief sat forward, placing her arms on the table and clasping her hands. The smile dripped off her face. "I can't guarantee he will kill faster, obviously, but the fact is he stopped killing after you disappeared. Since you've returned, he's killed once, which may or may not have been in response to your return. However, given that he's invaded your home and tried to kill you, he's lured you to a crime scene with a previous victim and tried to kill you again, I think that your return may have been the catalyst. I think it's clear he's escalating. We need to be prepared for his next move."

Leila mulled over the chief's words. As much as she didn't want to admit it, they made sense. TBK *had* been escalating. It was only a matter of time before the killer tried to come after her again. And this time, someone else might get in his way. Like Evie.

It also made sense that Brett would stay on hand in Sterling Ridge and lead his team. She'd been connected with law enforcement for several years. Long enough to recognize that someone had to be in charge and make the hard calls. That job usually fell to the lieutenants. In this case, it was obviously going to be Brett.

She peered at him from the corner of her eye. Despite his protest, she couldn't tell how he felt about the chief's orders. It was clear that he wasn't going to complain or ask for any sort of special treatment. But why should he? He was a man who did his duty. From what she'd seen so far, duty was paramount to him.

He caught her looking at him and gave her a brisk nod. "You'll be safe with Murphy. John's a stand-up guy, as fine a cop as I've ever met. You'll be in good hands with him."

She didn't doubt that, but she didn't know Sergeant Murphy. She knew Brett and felt safe with him. Oh, sure, she had gotten to know many of the officers in the past few days. They were all people she needed to start building a rapport with to enhance their working relationship.

Maybe it was a good thing that she wasn't going with Brett. The last thing she wanted was to start to rely on one person too much. She, and by extension Evie, would only be hurt in the long run. Hadn't she already learned that men couldn't be trusted to keep their promises in personal relationships? Hadn't her father and her husband taught her that it wasn't good to trust them unconditionally?

As soon as the briefing ended, Brett strode out of the room. Leila stared after him. Although she'd decided that she needed to keep her distance, the way he made it obvious that he had no such trouble stung. Clearly, the growing attraction was all on her side.

Katie hovered near her elbow.

"No use standing around. Let's go and collect Evie."

They went to the other conference room to get packed up and wait for Sergeant Murphy. The moment she opened the door, she knew Evie was in a temper. The child ran to the door and clung to her mother's legs. Leila rubbed her child's back, trying to soothe the tantrum she sensed approaching.

"I want to go home, Mommy. When can we go home?" Evie's lower lip pushed out. Her voice took on a whiny tone. The shine of tears in those big brown eyes made Leila want to cry, too. But she continued trying to calm her daughter.

"Sweetie, we're going on an adventure first. Katie wants us to come and meet some of her family. Won't that be fun?"

Evie thought about it. "Katie has horses."

Katie smothered a laugh at her side. "*Ja.* My family has two horses."

Evie's eyes brightened. "Do you ride them?"

"*Nee*, little one. They pull the buggy."

"Buggy?" Evie's nose scrunched up, like she was trying to figure out if Katie were making fun of her.

"*Ja.* My family doesn't drive cars. We use a horse and a buggy."

"You've seen them before, Evie." Leila brought out her phone and searched for a picture of an Amish horse and buggy. She pulled up one that looked like the buggies they saw around the area. She showed it to Evie. "See?"

"Is that Katie?" The little girl pointed to the Amish woman sitting in the buggy. Her head was turned away from the camera.

"*Nee*, Evie. My family doesn't take pictures of people. We don't believe in them." Katie pointed at the horse pulling the buggy. "One of our horses looks like that one."

"Pretty."

Phew. Tantrum avoided. Leila winked at Katie and began picking up all the toys. Katie and Evie gathered the crayons and put them back into the gallon bag. They zipped it shut just as the door opened. A young officer rapped twice and stuck his head into the room.

"Leila Britton?"

"Yes, you must be Sergeant Murphy." She walked over and shook his hand. "This is my daughter, Evie, and our friend Katie Weaver."

"Nice to meet y'all." His voice had the warm tint of a Southern accent, barely there. "The chief tells me I'm to be your personal escort this afternoon."

Leila liked his open manner. She could imagine him sitting around a campfire with a large family telling stories and jokes. He didn't have the intensity of Brett, but she could see his passion for his job.

Why had she thought of Brett again? She needed to get him out of her mind.

Sergeant Murphy chatted with them, making Evie laugh, all the way out to his cruiser.

Opening the rear door for her daughter, Leila was surprised. "Oh! You have a booster seat."

"Yes, ma'am. Lieutenant Talbot brought it to me when he heard I'd be taking you. He was very thorough in explaining how to fasten it in, too."

Her eyes stung, making her vision blurry. She blinked away the moisture. She'd thought he left because he didn't care. Instead, he'd rushed out to get the booster seat to protect her little girl.

Once Katie and Evie were buckled into the back seat, Sergeant Murphy held the front passenger door open for her. She sank into the seat, suddenly weary. If she could, she'd go to bed now and sleep for the next twelve hours.

Sergeant Murphy got in and started the car. He asked for Katie's address and plugged it into the GPS. They would go there first so Katie could get what they needed, then they would head to her cousin's house.

Leila jumped when someone knocked on her window. Swinging around, she half feared she'd see a black Grim Reaper mask staring back at her. Instead, Brett grinned in at her. She collapsed against her seat, a hand over her heart as if she could manually slow its rapid beat.

Brett motioned for her to roll down the window. When she did, he peeked into the back seat and gave Evie a thumbs-up. "I see the princess got her seat."

"She did. Thanks for thinking of it."

"I apologize I had to leave you with this guy."

Sergeant Murphy snickered. "Hey. I heard that."

"Seriously, you have my number. Call me if you need anything."

She doubted she'd do that, but she appreciated his concern. "I will. But I'm sure I won't need to."

He waited for an awkward second before stepping back and waving once. She watched his compelling stride until he entered the station again.

Sergeant Murphy kept up a stream of light and humorous conversation as they traveled toward Katie's Amish community. Suddenly his tone changed.

"What is this guy doing?" he muttered.

Leila flicked a glance to the van roaring up on the left. She froze when she saw the Grim Reaper mask. "That's him! It's TBK!"

Sergeant Murphy paled but didn't balk. He drew his gun and ordered them all to get down, then floored the accelerator.

The van driver shot at them. A metallic clang rang through the vehicle. Murphy called in to make a request for backup. When an exit came up, he spun off the interstate. He followed the curve around and stopped in the shadow of the bridge.

A slow-moving tractor rumbled close, temporarily blocking the van. It gave them a little wiggle room.

"You three, get out and hide in the bushes. I'll lead him away." Murphy said. "That tractor should block you for a second or two."

She wanted to protest, but her training told her to follow his orders. Evie sobbed as they pulled her from the car. The trio ran from the cruiser and hid as he'd told them to. He sped away.

They hadn't hidden a moment too soon. The van raced after the cruiser.

"Let's move," Leila said. "We need to get somewhere safer."

She remembered Brett's final words. Taking her phone,

she sent him a quick text. She didn't have time to talk with him. Right now they needed shelter.

The clip-clop of an approaching horse broke into her thoughts. Before she said anything, Katie ran in front of the buggy. The driver pulled on the reins to stop the horses. Leila didn't understand most of what was said. Katie had slipped into Pennsylvania Dutch, the language the Amish spoke in their homes. After a few frowns, the driver agreed.

Katie motioned them forward. "*Cumme.* He'll drive us to my *haus*."

Leila and Evie didn't wait but hopped into the back. Katie joined them. The older man continued driving. When she saw the van approaching from the other direction, she drew back from the windows. The van made a thumping sound when it sped past them.

"He's driving on a flat tire," the Amish man said. "*Ach.* He'll ruin it, for sure."

She held her peace, not wanting to announce in her daughter's hearing that the van driver was also a cold-blooded murderer out to get her. Evie knew she had an Aunt Tara who had gone to be with Jesus before she was born. Leila didn't plan to tell her the whole truth until she was old enough to handle the grim story.

She and Katie stayed away from the windows for another five minutes. Only once the van had disappeared in the distance and she was certain it hadn't turned to come back did she send Brett another text telling him where they were headed.

Brett's phone buzzed in his pocket. He'd missed a couple of texts while driving to meet with Carter. He pulled into the parking lot and slipped his phone from his pocket. The two texts he saw made the hair on his arms stand on end.

He immediately called the chief. "Murphy's in trouble. TBK attacked them en route to Katie's."

"He called it in, but there's been no word from him since."

"I got a text from Leila. He let them out and took the heat. An Amish man picked them up. They're safe, but I'm concerned about Sergeant Murphy."

"I want you to head to his last known location. Lieutenant Flint, too."

"Got it."

When Carter pulled up, Brett gave him the message. Soon, both cruisers were on the way. When they approached the exit where Murphy had dropped off the women, Brett slowed. There was no sign of them, but he didn't expect to see them.

The radio burst to life. The dispatcher called out a request for an ambulance and the local fire department. She also said the police were on the way. Chief Kaiser must have called it in. He didn't know how he'd missed it.

Too much going on inside his brain, he reasoned.

At least she'd called for an ambulance and not the coroner. So there was still the possibility that Sergeant Murphy had survived.

When the traffic slowed and began to bottleneck, he knew they were getting closer. Nothing disrupted the flow of traffic like a gapers' block. Fortunately, nothing cleared the way like police sirens and lights. The line of slow-moving cars steered to the side of the two-lane street. He barreled past with Carter on his bumper.

He continued along the road. In the distance, a cloud of black smoke rose in the air. Brett's fingers tightened on the steering wheel. His stomach felt as if the protein shake he'd drunk an hour ago had turned into cement in his gut.

Please, God. Murphy's young. He has so much life ahead of him. Let him be okay.

Sergeant Murphy, like every person who earned his badge, knew and accepted that his career choice might cost him his life. Brett, too, knew someday he might die in the line of duty. That didn't mean it was an easy thing to face.

He kept steadily praying while he drove. Five minutes later, he saw the cruiser where it had crashed into the guardrail. Flames shot from the engine. A bystander had stopped and was spraying the engine with a fire extinguisher. His vehicle, parked in front of the cruiser, bore a volunteer fire department sticker.

Flipping his blinker on, Brett drove off the main part of the street and parked behind the cruiser, putting some distance between the two vehicles. He extinguished the siren but left the lights on and the engine running, in case he needed to leave fast. Carter's cruiser pulled directly behind him.

On the side of the road, Sergeant Murphy lay in the grass. A couple of men were already hovering around him.

Brett and Carter hurried over to him. Brett's mouth and throat were like sandpaper, they were so dry. He tried to swallow.

"Glad you made it, guys," Murphy drawled, his voice slurred.

He was alive. One of the men held a folded towel against Murphy's side. Taking in the latex gloves and the bag at his side, Brett concluded he was either a doctor or a paramedic.

The man barely flicked his gaze at them. "He's been shot. I obviously can't operate here."

A doctor, then.

"The ambulance is on the way. I don't know what happened to the women and the child he's telling me about."

The man's lips tightened until a white ring encircled them. "I can't look for them, but I sent my son to comb the area."

Murphy groaned. "I had to send them out, Lieutenant. I knew he wanted to kill Leila. Was I wrong? Did I—"

Brett crouched down next to Murphy. "You were smart, Sergeant. You saved their lives. They're safe, all of them."

Sergeant Murphy sighed and closed his eyes. "Good. I couldn't live with myself if they died because I didn't protect them."

Brett settled a calming hand on his colleague's shoulder. "You did good. You protected them by making yourself the target. I'm putting your name in for commendation. You've earned it."

Murphy's lips turned up in a weary smile. "That's nice. My mom will be proud."

"She should be. She's raised a brave son."

Carter joined them, with a teenager at his side. He addressed the doctor. "I brought your son back."

"I'm just glad the women are safe," the doctor replied.

A shiver slid through Brett. Were they, though? He knew where they were headed. But he had no idea if they had made it. He sent Leila a text. A few seconds later, he got a message that it had failed to send. Probably because of the limited service in Katie's area. And Amish had no phones. He'd have to go out to Katie's house to assure himself that Leila, Katie and Evie were alive and well.

Little Evie must be traumatized by the events of the day. How did one explain to a kid that they had to flee from a car and hide? At least her mother was with her. Brett needed to finish here and go to them.

But he had a colleague to tend to first. And a crime scene.

"I don't suppose either of you saw what happened?" Carter's gaze shifted from the doctor to his son.

"I did," a third voice answered.

It was the man with the fire extinguisher. "I was a few cars behind him," he said, pointing to Murphy.

"Yes? Go on." Carter had his phone out to make notes.

"I saw a van speed up beside the cop car. I thought to myself, *what an idiot. He's going to get a ticket.* I'm not gonna lie, I wanted that to happen. I have no patience with reckless drivers."

Brett kept his hands clasped together. The temptation to make a hurry-up gesture coursed through him. He tensed, keeping his hands still. He'd been a cop long enough to know you had to let people talk in their own way. Rushing him might make him leave out details they needed.

"Anyway, then I saw something flash. It wasn't until the cop car swerved that I realized the driver had shot the cop! I was shocked. But this guy—" he pointed at Murphy "—shot back. Hit the back tire. He was driving with a flat tire in minutes."

How long could someone drive at full speed on a rim? Not long. Brett leaped to his feet, his fingers on the radio.

"The suspect is driving a van with a blown tire. He might need to bail and go on foot. He's dangerous, so it's possible he'll attempt to steal a vehicle."

Dispatch responded immediately. "Backup is on the way. The nearby precincts have been alerted and are joining in the hunt."

Brett looked at the witness. "I don't suppose you saw the man driving the van?"

He shook his head. "No, sir. I was too far behind to see anything like that."

"I didn't think so, but I needed to ask." Not that it would

have mattered had he seen him. Brett already knew from Leila's text it was TBK.

"He was wearing a mask," Sergeant Murphy groaned. "One of those Grim Reaper things. You wouldn't have seen his face."

Brett nodded. "I know, buddy. Listen, you just rest and get better. We'll handle it."

An ambulance going in the opposite direction did a precise U-turn and pulled up alongside them. Brett and Carter backed out of the way to allow the paramedics to work.

"We're down two officers now," Carter stated, his voice hushed. "Ryan will grouse about it, but the chief won't let him back until he's cleared."

"I'm not ashamed to admit that I'll be glad when he's back. We're in over our heads, and we still have a serial killer after Leila." Brett shoved his hands into his uniform pockets.

"Look, Brett, you know where Katie lives, right?"

"Yeah. At least, I have her address in my GPS. And I know the general area."

Carter nodded once, his mouth a firm line. "You go and check on our photographer. I'll wait here for the crime scene unit and take care of getting all the statements in."

"You sure?" Even as he asked, Brett started backing away toward his vehicle.

"Yeah. Go."

Brett didn't need to be told again. He fled back to his car, eager to be on his way. He wouldn't be able to focus until he saw with his own eyes that Leila and Evie were alive and well.

However, he knew once this case ended, he'd have to let them go. Not only because of his own baggage. Leila had had enough trauma in her life. He knew there was a connection between them, a spark he had never experienced before. But she had already lost a sister tragically, and a husband. He couldn't ask her to join her life with his. And he couldn't step away from being a cop. It was who he was, who God had called him to be.

And obedience to God must come first.

Even if it meant letting his own heart's desire walk away.

TEN

By the time they reached Katie's home, Leila's body ached and her muscles were stiff from hunching against the side of the buggy. Even after she and Katie had decided the van had disappeared, she still quaked every time she heard a motor approaching.

The driver let them off at the bottom of the Weaver driveway. He and Katie held a soft conversation, but Leila wasn't able to listen in. She tried to lift her daughter without waking her, but the child stirred in her arms.

"It's okay, Evie. Mommy's got you."

"I'm a big girl, Mommy. Babies get carried."

Leila closed her eyes briefly. "That's not always true, Evie. It's a really long driveway."

Evie leaned to look over her mother's shoulder. "Okay. You can carry me."

They hadn't gone very far before a new concern rose in Evie's mind.

"I'm hungry, Mommy." Evie yawned, showing all of her perfect white teeth. "I didn't get my afternoon snack."

"I will get it for you soon, sweetie. It's in my bag."

Leila packed light, as a rule, but having no idea how long they would be gone or where they were going meant she had to be prepared for whatever situation they found themselves in. She had snacks, changes of clothes for various weather conditions, toys and art supplies that her daughter could use without electricity.

She wasn't looking forward to telling Evie that she couldn't watch her favorite cartoon for the next few days. However, Evie would get over it. She was resilient, as children tended to be. It wouldn't hurt her to spend a few days living simply with no internet or television. At four, she hadn't discovered video games yet. Leila didn't plan on those entering the picture for years, if ever. She remained undecided on their potential for harm.

She hoped she didn't have to give up her phone. She glanced at her smart watch. Her phone and the watch were the full spread of her electronic devices, other than the computer she used for work. Out here in the Amish community, she wouldn't have a landline in the house. Although the barn might have one. Otherwise, her phone was her only way to contact anyone.

Like Brett. Or the police. If she had to give that up…

She felt the isolation closing in on her. Taking a deep breath, she held it in for a moment, trying to slow her heartbeat.

It was going to be fine, she told herself.

God, I know I haven't been a fan of Yours for a while. I'm trying to find my way back. Please help me get through this and protect Evie. And Katie. And Brett.

Why had she tacked his name on the end? He wasn't even with them. As far as she knew, she wouldn't see him again until the next time they worked on a case together. And she needed to deal with that.

First, though, she needed to survive this one.

If only she could keep her little girl safe from the evil stalking them now.

She turned when she realized Katie hadn't come with them. She was still talking with the driver. She didn't want to show up at the door without Katie. Not knowing how long it would take, she set Evie down for a bit.

A minute later, Katie backed away from the buggy and waved at the driver. He flicked his wrist and the horse started off at a slow trot. Leila held Evie's hand, waiting for their friend.

"Let me take one of those bags, Leila."

Gladly, she surrendered one of the totes to the Amish woman.

"Umph. These are heavy! Let's go to the *haus*. I can introduce you to my *mamm* and *daed* and my *bruders*. Then we can talk about what to do next."

"I'm not looking forward to this, Katie." Leila hefted the straps higher on her shoulder. Then she picked up Evie again.

"Oh? Why not? My family is kind."

"I don't doubt that. But even though this is your suggestion, I still feel guilty. I am literally bringing danger to your house."

Katie clicked her tongue. "You are in danger. It's not your fault. You didn't cause it."

She knew that. But in her mind she still had an inkling of worry that she was the cause. What if she had done something in her past to anger someone enough to kill? Even as she thought it, her entire being rejected the idea. She could not think of a single instance in her life where she had gone out of her way to antagonize someone or bully them. She never cheated; she tried to always be honest, yet fair.

Still, the other women all resembled her, even if it was only in coloring and body type. They had been innocent victims.

By the time they reached the house, Evie's had begun to whine.

It broke Leila's heart. Her baby had been through a lot.

Katie's mother was inside the house making dinner. Her jaw dropped when her daughter entered, followed by Leila. Leila couldn't blame her for the suspicious way her eyes moved over them—a strange *Englisch* woman and a cranky four-year-old. "Katie? What is happening?"

"*Mamm.* Is *Daed* in the barn?"

"Ja."

"I need to speak with you both. I'll go get him." Katie turned and fled out the door. It banged shut behind her.

Leila gritted her teeth. She couldn't recall a more awkward situation. When her daughter squirmed in her arms, she gently set her on her feet.

Evie sniffed the air. "Mommy, I'm hungry."

Leila's face burned. She opened her mouth to tell her daughter to be patient for a few more minutes.

"*Ack!* Poor *kind*! I have sweet rolls. Would you like one, *liebling*?" Katie's mother grabbed an aluminum tray filled with sweet rolls topped with a luscious maple frosting. "I made these this morning."

Evie grinned. Still, she looked back at her mother. "Mommy, can I have one?"

How could she say no? "Mrs. Weaver—"

"Ada, please. Only the *Englisch* say Mrs."

Well, she was *Englisch*. But she didn't correct the woman. "Ada, then. I don't want to be any trouble."

"*Nee* trouble. If she's hungry, of course she may eat one. Let me get the *kind* a plate."

Evie didn't need to hear any more. She scooted onto the bench at the table and waited, her eyes wide and ravenous.

Ada set the treat in front of her. Evie stuck her fork in it, then stopped.

"Thank you, Mrs. Ada."

Both women chuckled. "*Gut*, eat up, little one." She turned to Leila. "Katie will be back with David soon. We will talk then, *ja*? Why tell the same story twice."

"I agree."

Five minutes later, Katie, her father and a young man around Katie's age, probably her brother, entered the house. "Leila, this is my *daed*, David, and my *bruder* Jonah. And my *mamm*, Ada."

Leila greeted them, shifting her weight from one foot to another. She let Katie take charge of telling all the details. After all, this was her family. She waited for them to tell her to take her child and leave.

"We can't get you to Vera's *haus* today, Katie." David stroked his beard. "It's too far for the buggy. You'll need a driver."

"Can I go, too?" Jonah grabbed a sweet roll out of the pan and tore off a huge chunk with his teeth.

"*Ja.* You can *cumme*," David said. "Katie, call for a driver. See if one can take you tomorrow morning."

Leila blinked. And just like that, they had accepted her into the house, even with all the trouble that came with her. She'd never seen generosity this openly displayed before.

"You don't mind? Someone is after me."

"*Gott* will provide." Ada gathered Evie's plate and fork and brought them to the dishpan. "It's time for this one to clean up. She's sticky."

Evie grinned, a ring of frosting around her mouth. "It was yummy."

Leila could already see the bond of affection developing between the child and Katie's mother. She blinked rapidly.

If only her mom had lived to see Evie. Maybe she would have regained some of her zest for life if she'd had a granddaughter to love.

She shoved the thought away. Wondering about what might have happened never helped.

Ada broke into her reverie. "If you are trying to avoid notice, you might want to dress Plain."

Katie nodded. "I hoped we could scrounge together clothes for them."

Despite the situation, Leila smiled. *Scrounge* was a word Katie had picked up from her. She hoped her mother wouldn't mind.

Ada narrowed her eyes and pursed her lips, scanning both Leila and Evie. "*Ja.* I don't think that will be hard. Katie, your dresses will be too long, ain't so? But your older *schwester*'s clothes might fit."

"Susannah married two years ago," Katie whispered to Leila. "Some of her clothes are still here. We'll see if they fit you."

While Ada scraped up a couple of outfits, Katie started in on their hair. Evie giggled while her hair was braided and then pinned to her head. Ada walked into the room a few minutes later with several dresses in her arms.

"This one belonged to my Katie when she was young."

When Evie saw the dress, she pouted. "I like shorts."

Leila stepped in. "Let's make it a game, sweetie. Mommy will be wearing a dress and a *kapp*, too."

The child wasn't convinced, but she allowed them to place a black *kapp* on her head. Leila got a white one.

"I want a white *kapp*, too," Evie protested.

"White is for grown-ups. Black is for *kinder*," Ada informed her.

For some reason, Evie didn't argue with her.

The dress Ada offered to Leila was olive green. Leila wasn't happy that it had no pockets until Katie handed her the apron that went over the dress. It was the same color.

"We're not allowed to have pockets in our dresses, but our aprons have them."

She placed her phone in the pocket. She'd keep it there for now. She might not have any battery power left in it before long.

Within an hour, the family sat down for supper. After the meal was done, Katie left to go help her aunt with something before they left in the morning. Evie practically fell asleep at the table, so Ada helped Leila put her to bed.

Around eight o'clock, Leila was ready to declare herself ready for bed, too.

"There's a police car in the driveway," Jonah announced.

Heart pounding in her chest, Leila hurried to the window. It was a sedan, not an SUV like Brett drove. For a moment, her hope deflated. Then the passenger door opened and Brett stepped out into the early evening.

Joy burst inside Leila. The weariness dropped from her. Without thought, she shoved open the door, ran down the three front steps and rushed to Brett. He had enough time to turn and face her before she threw her arms around him.

Brett staggered back two steps until he hit the side of Michaela's car. Shocked to find himself holding an Amish woman in his arms, he started to push her away from him.

The woman quickly dropped her arms and jumped back. Under the white *kapp*, a familiar face looked at him for a moment before her she blushed scarlet and dropped her gaze.

"Sorry. I shouldn't have done that."

"Leila?" He stepped closer and placed a finger under her chin to raise her face. "I didn't recognize you!"

She grinned impishly, her cheeks still a little pink. "Isn't that the point? What are you doing here?" The humor bled out of her expression. "Oh! How is Sergeant Murphy?"

"He was shot, but he'll make a complete recovery."

"Good."

"As to why I'm here, well, the chief wants someone with you. Since Murphy is injured, she decided I should come."

He might have insisted and she'd given in. He refused to tell Leila that, though.

"Where's your car?"

He jerked a thumb back toward the sedan he'd nearly fallen on when she charged at him. "Michaela gave me a ride here. If I'm going undercover with you, I can't have a police cruiser parked at an Amish house. I meant to get here earlier, but the chief had some last-minute things I needed to do before I was free to go."

"Anything I should know?"

"Well, the silver car our perp drove the first time he attacked you has been found. It was stolen. There is a dark van that was reported stolen in the past week, too. Since this one had its rear tire shot out, I'm thinking we'll find it on the side of the road soon and he'll have to steal another car."

She scrunched up her nose, looking absurdly adorable in her Amish dress. "Does he not have his own wheels?"

"Maybe. Or maybe he likes seeing how bad he can be. How many laws he can break."

"Lieutenant Talbot," Michaela called. "I just got a call from the chief. I need to get back to Sterling Ridge, sir. If I can."

"Let me check on things here first." He turned back to Leila. "I didn't expect to find you here. I thought I'd get the address from Katie's family and then we'd drive out there. But you're here. What's the plan?"

"We're using a driver tomorrow morning."

"You can stay tonight, Brett," Katie called out.

Huh. He hadn't noticed her approach. Leila had captured all his attention.

"I can catch a ride with you tomorrow morning?"

"*Ja.* For sure."

He went back and grabbed his things and Evie's booster seat from the cruiser. Michaela waved and drove off after he promised to check in with the station at regular intervals.

Katie's family took the news of his addition with calm grace. He was promptly given a room to himself and provided with a hot meal. The unrest that had seethed through his veins all day left him once he saw Leila and Evie were well. He chose not to think about that for the time being. He had accepted that nothing could come of their attraction. But the feeling of her in his arms… He wished he could have the privilege to hold her one more time.

Wednesday morning dawned hot and humid. Brett hopped out of bed and got ready for the day in the clothes David had found for him. It felt very strange not to have pockets. Or to have his gun on him. He'd have to find a way around that one. If he tucked it into his waistband and left the shirt untucked… No. He'd stand out too much. But if he was going to protect Leila, he needed to carry.

For now, he hid his Glock in his bag.

When he heard voices in the kitchen, he joined the rest of the family.

"*Gut* morning, Brett," Ada greeted him. She set a plate stacked high with pancakes on the table and gestured for him to sit. He hadn't had homemade pancakes in years. His stomach growled, making them all laugh.

"Good morning." He waited while they prayed, then dug in. The pancakes were delicious.

"The driver will be here at ten." Katie took a delicate bite.

"Can you be ready to leave by then?" he asked Leila.

"Yes. As long as Evie cooperates." She rolled her eyes at her daughter. The little girl wore a grin and a syrup mustache. He hid his smile in a napkin. The kid was too cute for her own good.

After breakfast Brett asked Leila if she wanted to go for a little walk outside. They would stay on the property, but they were going to be cramped together in a car for almost two hours. "If you want a chance to stretch your legs, this is it."

She hesitated, her eyes sliding toward Evie.

"Don't worry about her," Katie assured them. "*Mamm* and I will watch her until you get back. It's a *gut* idea for you to go and get some exercise now. Oh, and I called the driver. We're to meet him at the normal spot at ten."

Brett looked around. "Normal spot?"

Ada nodded. "Our driveway has too many ruts for some of the *Englisch* vehicles. So we always have them meet us at my cousin's *haus*."

She gave him the address.

"Okay." He wasn't feeling too sure about this change, but it was too late to alter it. "I don't like the idea of all of us going there in a big group." He looked at Katie and her parents. "Can you take Evie in a buggy and meet us there?"

"Brett!"

He placed a hand on Leila's shoulder. "He's expecting you to have Evie. Even if your disguise fails, he might not recognize you without your daughter. And there's no way either Katie or Ada could be you."

Ada was older and had a larger frame. And Katie was much taller than her.

"So you're saying she might be safer with them?"

"Exactly."

"If I drive them in the buggy," David said, "we'll just look like any Plain family out for a drive."

"Ja." Ada nodded.

Leila allowed herself to be convinced. Then she and Brett went outside for their walk. At first, they talked about inconsequential matters. Mundane small talk just to pass the time. Leila's gaze kept straying back to the house. When the others left with Evie and nothing happened, her shoulders finally relaxed.

"Told you it was safer for her."

"So you did. Why did you become a cop?" she asked suddenly.

He stumbled. His past wasn't something he liked to talk about.

"You don't have to tell me." She apologized. "I shouldn't have asked."

"No, it's a common enough question. It's just that… I just don't tell people about my childhood."

She had shared her past with him, though. He realized he wanted her to know. No one knew except for Carter.

"I'll be honest. I didn't always want to be a cop. In fact, when I was kid, my only dream was to leave home and never look back."

Leila was a good listener. She didn't interrupt or act uncomfortable. She was a calm presence. Someone he instinctively trusted.

"See, I grew up with an alcoholic father, one who was abusive. When I was in my teens, I'd often put myself between him and my mom."

"That was brave," she murmured.

"Maybe." He wasn't sure about that. Suddenly, the emotions rushed out of him. "I was so mad at her. I was the kid, and I had to protect her. But she never protected me."

"That must have been difficult." Her tone held no judgment.

"Yeah. It was. When I was eighteen, he went too far, and she died in my arms."

Her hand reached for his. It wasn't a romantic gesture, but a soothing sign of care. He gripped her hand, treasuring the contact. He shook his head, trying to reassert control over his emotions. "He's in jail now. I don't expect him to ever get out."

"Have you visited him?"

"Nope. Not going to, either."

She was silent for a few moments. "You know, I stopped believing in God's love after my sister died. But these last few days, I've sensed Him again."

"Oh, yeah?" He hoped she wasn't going to tell him he needed to forgive his dad. He knew it but wasn't ready to go there yet.

"I've missed having faith." She paused, then continued in a low voice. "I've also missed my dad, but I don't know what to do about that one."

That was all she said. She didn't tell him how to act, or what to do. He let the rich silence linger between them. Somehow, in just three days, they had come to the place where secrets they had hidden from the world could be safely shared.

He didn't want to destroy what they had found. But he didn't know how it could last.

They finished their walk.

"We should go in and get ready to meet the others." She glanced at her watch.

"You shouldn't wear a watch here."

Leila scowled at him but duly removed her watch and shoved it in her apron pocket. "I'll keep it here."

He didn't point out to her that in a day or so, she might not have any charge left. He really didn't want to remind her that she might be stuck at someone else's house for a while. She was so independent, he doubted she'd care for the reminder.

Still, he had to grin at her spunk.

Together, they walked to the back door of the house. While she went to clean up, he went into his room and gathered his things. At the last moment, he untucked his shirt in the back and put his holster on under it. They might be hiding in Amish country, but he was still a Sterling Ridge police officer, and Leila and her daughter were under his protection.

A few minutes later, he met her in the living room. She was looking around, probably making sure she had all of Evie's things. The hum of a motor interrupted his thoughts. Instinctively, he pulled her back against the wall in the hallway. None of the windows, including the large picture window in the living room, had drapes over them. She didn't protest. Her breathing sped up.

Brett casually stepped to the entranceway and leaned over far enough to peer into the living room and out the front window. At first he saw nothing. Then, as he watched, a dark van drove by.

"He changed the tire," he muttered.

"Is that him?"

"Yeah. We need to leave as soon as possible."

But how would they make it to the meeting place without being seen?

ELEVEN

"What do we do?" Leila hissed. "My daughter is at Katie's cousin's house, waiting for us."

She clutched his arm as if she could force answers from him.

Brett watched the road. "We'll have to get there without being noticed. We obviously can't take the main road."

"Brett! I need to get to my daughter!" Didn't he understand? Her daughter was with Katie and her family. She knew enough about the Amish to know that they did not believe in fighting. Not even in defense of someone else. If something happened, how would they protect her little girl? Why had she agreed to separate?

Brett's hand covered hers. He tightened his fingers around hers until she looked up at him. His blue eyes were steady. She forced herself to pull in a deep breath.

"Leila, I know it's hard. I know you're worried about Evie. But I truly believe that she is safer with them than she is with you right now. Whoever this guy is, he is looking for you. You already know that he knows what you look like. There is very little chance that he will mistake Katie for you."

"But what if he knows enough about me to think he'll use Katie as bait?"

"Which is why we need to leave here. He hasn't pulled into the driveway, which tells me he has an idea of where Katie lives, but he does not know her exact house. And I have worked with the Amish enough to know they're not going to tell anybody who comes by where somebody lives."

He did have a good point about the fact that the van had not pulled into the Weaver driveway yet. So there was a chance that whoever this killer was, he might know a little bit about her life, but not everything.

But he knew enough that it worried her.

"Even if you're right," she said, "it's already twenty minutes after nine. We're supposed to meet them at ten."

"They won't leave without us."

"I know, but what if we're late and they decide to search for us? Then we'll all be wandering about, vulnerable."

"What we need to do is go out the back of the barn and make our way to the meeting point."

She started to nod, then she heard voices.

"Oh, sure, I know where they live," an elderly woman said. "Right across the street, in that house. The white one with the horse grazing in the field."

"Thank you, ma'am. You have been very helpful." The male voice was smooth and clear. Cheerful. Not a voice anyone would connect with a serial killer.

Leila held her breath as heavy footsteps pounded up the Weaver driveway and stepped onto the front porch. She glared at her protector.

"You said no would give them away," she hissed at Brett. "He's out there on the porch."

"Did you hear her voice? She wasn't Amish." He listened for a moment. The killer was trying to jimmy the lock. "Quietly, we'll walk to the back door."

She nodded to show she understood. Barely lifting her feet off the ground, she moved one step at a time. It felt like they were moving in slow motion. Every step of the way, she felt Brett's breath on the back of her neck. When he'd come downstairs, she's seen the shape of his gun under the linen shirt, and now she was grateful for it.

"Once you're outside, do you think you can keep walking to the cousin's house?" he asked her.

"What? By myself?" She had to remind herself to whisper.

"Yes. This is the perfect opportunity to wait and ambush him."

She didn't want to. She really didn't want to go alone. But he was right.

She opened her mouth, then stopped. She sniffed. "Smoke."

He stopped. Ran back to peer out the window. Then he ran to the kitchen. "He's set both porches on fire."

"We're trapped?" She'd been so afraid of death by drowning. It never occurred to her to fear death by being trapped in a house on fire. Thank God Evie wasn't here.

"No. Jonah gave me the tour last night. We'll go out through the attic. There's a trapdoor. Then a tree. Follow me."

She didn't have much choice. Already the smoke was filtering into the house. She pulled the apron up and held it over her mouth and nose. She shoved her hand into the pocket to verify her inhaler was there. It was. She patted it to reassure herself, then followed him up the narrow staircase, coughing into the apron.

"I don't know why Jonah showed me this. I think he thought it was cool. Which it is. I, however, prefer to think it was providential." He placed his hands on a large panel on the ceiling and shoved it sideways. It slid away, creating an entrance. She could see the low beams and slanted roof.

Brett helped her into the attic, then dragged the panel shut again. "We'll keep the smoke out." There was a small window at one end of the attic. They had to weave their way through boxes, crates and wooden chairs. A couple of times, her toe caught on something and she would have pitched forward if it weren't for Brett standing in front of her, guiding her along.

When she reached the window, she took a moment to use her inhaler. Then she looked out the window and her belly took a dive.

About six inches away from the window, a thick branch extended to a large tree. Another branch on the other side ended near the roof of the barn.

"You want me to climb not one but two branches?" She wasn't afraid of heights, but she didn't exactly have the necessary skills to walk a tightrope, either.

"It's the only way out."

She sniffed. The smoke smell had thickened. The temperature in the attic seemed to have risen at least ten degrees since they had entered. They were running out of time to escape the fire.

Brett opened the window. There was no screen in it. Going back into the middle of the room, he grabbed a large chest and tugged it over to the window.

"You can stand on this."

Drawing in a deep, calming breath, she told herself she could do this. Accepting his hand, she scrambled onto the chest, half-afraid it wouldn't hold her weight. When nothing broke, she took another bracing breath and leaned out the window. Flames raked the side of the house. She heard a noise behind her and turned. Brett had his phone out and was dialing 911.

"Go," he told her. "I'll be right behind you."

Leila hefted herself onto the window ledge and inched her way out and onto the tree limb, praying that she and Brett would both come out the other end of this adventure alive.

If there was one thing Brett admired, it was true courage. The kind where someone was terrified of something but did it anyway. Exactly like the way Leila was slowly making her way across the tree limb on her hands and knees.

He'd seen her fear. Her desperation to find another way. But when it really mattered, she buckled down and did it anyway.

If she'd been standing there still, he would have kissed her.

He wiped that image from his mind, although he doubted it would stay away. He'd held her in his arms. He knew how tempting she was.

He levered himself up and squeezed through the small window. Unlike Leila, who was small and trim, he had the build of a wrestler who had become a Marine and trained hard daily. He had to work to get his shoulders through the narrow opening. The shirt the Weavers had lent him ripped. He'd probably left a layer of skin on the sill.

It could not be helped. And a little bit of pain was a fair price if it meant both he and Leila would escape with their lives.

When his full weight settled on the branch, it dipped alarmingly. He stayed put for a moment, feeling as though a huge bull's-eye was on him, and waited until she reached the trunk of the tree. Where the branch met the trunk, a sort of bowl had formed. Leila stepped onto the platform in the middle of the tree.

Brett made his way to her, the branch swaying under his weight. With each inch he gained, he held his breath, waiting to hear the crack beneath him that would precede his fall to the ground.

It was a long way down.

Finally, he reached the trunk. He clambered off the branch and onto the platform. Relief that they were both alive poured through him. Without thinking, he tugged her to him and held on tight. Just for two seconds. Then he released her. Bending down, he whispered into her ear.

"We're only halfway there, honey. Can you see where you jump off onto the roof?"

She shivered. Then she nodded. "Yes, I see it."

"Climb off the branch and go over to the far back left corner. There's a ladder hanging from the roof to the ground."

"I can do this."

"I know you can. God bless. I will follow you."

He glanced around quickly to make sure the killer wasn't in sight. When he saw no one, he gave her a soft nudge. Leila moved out onto the second branch. When she wobbled a bit, he held his breath. He couldn't help her, and if he called to her or distracted her, he feared she would fall.

Come on, Leila. Just a few more steps.

She reached the end and jumped lightly to the roof. The moment she hit the surface, she dropped and crawled to the end, keeping as low as she could.

Brett was ready to move onto the branch when he heard something. Flattening himself against the trunk, he reached around and removed his gun from the holster. Peering around the leaves that kept him hidden, he saw a shadow moving around the side of the house, careful to stay clear of the flames that continued to creep up the wood frame.

Finally, a distant siren cut through the air.

By the time the fire engines arrived, there would not be much of the house left to salvage. But he knew the Amish would come together and rebuild the Weaver home. Any possessions they had would be replaced by the community.

No lives were lost. His Amish friends would say the things didn't matter.

He still felt bad that the killer had torched their house to get to Leila. He probably had meant to smoke her out, seeing how he preferred to drown or strangle his victims.

Not today.

From where Brett stood, he could see that Leila had reached the side of the barn. Suddenly, he wanted to warn her to stay there and not go down the ladder yet. He almost got his phone and texted. But what if she didn't have her notifications silenced? That simple noise could lead the killer right to her.

The sirens were closer now. The killer made an aggravated grunt and ran toward the road. Brett leaned as far as he safely could, determined to keep an eye on his departure.

Once he was no longer in sight, Brett ventured out onto the second branch. He didn't dare try to rush. Even though the killer had fled the house at the sound of the sirens, it didn't mean he had completely left the scene.

Brett had a feeling he would stick around and attempt to grab Leila.

Gripping the branch, he pulled himself the final few feet and then dropped to the top of the roof.

A shot whistled past his shoulder. He flattened himself and army crawled deeper in. Twisting around, he tried to get a look at the killer's position. A second shot had him crouching down to the roof once more.

Brett pulled his own weapon. But he couldn't shoot. He didn't have a clear sight of his target, and there was a chance of hitting innocent citizens.

He needed to get to Leila.

He replaced the Glock in its holster and army crawled the rest of the way across the roof. She had not gone down the ladder completely. When she saw him, he motioned her to climb back up.

"The police and fire department are on the way. We'll wait here. If we keep down, he can't see us from the ground. I know because I looked when Jonah showed me earlier."

"How do we get to the others?"

"We'll have the police give us a ride over." He reached over and softly brushed a curl off her cheek. "You were amazing. Do you know that?"

She smiled. "Yeah? I think we made a good team."

Fifteen minutes later, the area swarmed with police. Brett talked with the officer in charge while another sat with Leila in the cruiser. He described the fire and how it started.

"Did you happen to get a look at him?"

"I didn't, but I know he asked one of the neighbors, an elderly woman across the street, for directions to the house. She might be able to describe him." As irritated as he was about not getting a look at the criminal, he hoped that this might finally give them a break in the case. If the woman could describe the man she'd seen, they could get a forensic artist to talk to her. Then they could send the sketch out to all the area precincts. Maybe the killer was already in the criminal database.

He doubted it would be that easy.

He started to feel uneasy about the woman the killer had talked to.

"I think we should go check on her now," he urged the other lieutenant, whose badge read Lieutenant Reynolds. "I have a bad feeling about this. I mean, she's a witness."

The other man's face shifted. "Let's go now."

After making sure that Leila was guarded, they went over to the house. They knocked twice.

"Ma'am. It's the police. Can we talk with you?"

No response. Lieutenant Reynolds tried the knob; it was unlocked. Reynolds's men went in and fanned out, weapons drawn.

"Sir!" Brett followed Lieutenant Reynolds. They found the elderly woman in a recliner, a paperback on her lap, a bullet hole in her chest.

Brett sighed. She had tried to help a stranger. She didn't deserve to die for it. It didn't help when they learned she was a widow with three grown children and seven grandchildren, two more on the way.

No child should learn that their parent had died this way.

When he had finished with Lieutenant Reynolds, he made his way back to Leila.

She blinked back a tear when he told her about the woman. Surprisingly, though, her first words weren't about how it was their fault.

"Don't you dare blame yourself," she ordered him. "You have done nothing but try and outmaneuver this maniac every step of the way. You can't see all his moves, or who he'll hurt. All you can do is try to find him and lock him away."

Leaning in, he kissed her cheek.

Her eyes flared wide-open. "What was that for?"

"That was because I was letting myself go to a very dark place. And you pulled me out."

She gave him a cheeky grin. "I get it. You like to brood."

"I don't like it. I just sometimes get into a mood, and it helps to have someone there to talk me out of it."

He didn't have many people who did that for him. Until Leila entered his world, Carter had been his main support system. He knew any of his colleagues would take a bullet for him in a heartbeat. But only Carter knew the dark corners of his soul. And now Leila did, also.

It felt good having someone else know him that well. Even if her presence in his life was temporary.

"I'll be glad to help talk you out of your moods, Brett. You are a good man. Remember that."

"I'll try. We should go meet with the Weavers. They need to learn what happened to their house."

She tensed.

"You just lectured me about blaming myself for that woman's death. Don't you blame yourself for the fire. The same person responsible for her murder is responsible for the house. At least the house will be rebuilt."

"Really?"

"Oh, yeah. The Amish do that. When a house burns down or some catastrophe happens, no one bands together like they do."

The world would be a different place if they did.

He had his work cut out for him. He had to find a killer who no one ever seemed to see and protect a woman and child. At the same time, he had to keep reminding himself that Leila was not part of his life and that he couldn't afford to fall for her, no matter how she made him feel.

He had a feeling he had already lost that battle.

TWELVE

The driver Katie had hired was hopping mad by the time they arrived at the pickup place. Katie and her family, though, didn't seem bothered by the delay.

Brett hated to be the bearer of bad news. He approached the small group waiting for them.

"I don't have all day, you know, right?" the driver flared. He was a young man in his early twenties. "I have stuff planned for today. You said ten. It's almost eleven now!"

"Dude," Brett said, annoyed. Hadn't this kid learned yet that sometimes life happens? "It's not their fault. Something happened. I will pay you for the extra time, if that helps."

He leaned back against his seat, still grumbling. "I expect to be paid for it."

Brett turned his back on the fuming man and led the group away from him so he couldn't hear what he said. Then he faced Katie's folks. "David. Ada. I apologize. The man who is after Leila found her. He was looking for Katie. I'm not sure how he got her name, but obviously he knew she was connected with Leila. The lady across the road identified your house. I regret to inform you that he shot her."

"Oh! Is she dead?" Ada asked, her voice quivering.

Brett nodded. "Yes, ma'am. I'm afraid she is."

David reached out and wrapped a comforting arm around his wife. Brett cleared his throat. He wasn't done delivering the bad news.

"I'm afraid he also set your house on fire to try and get to us." Brett was no one to TBK. Whoever this guy was, he wanted Leila and didn't care who he hurt to get to her.

"Poor Nia!" Ada wept. "She was a *gut* woman. Always ready to help out."

"*Ja.* She was."

It never failed to amaze him. He had just told this family that their house had burned down, and they acted as if it didn't even matter. He envied that sort of disconnect from material possessions. How much easier life would be if people weren't so concerned about what they owned. Their entire focus was on the woman who had lost her life. He agreed with their priorities, that was for certain.

"I'm so sorry, Ada. David," Leila murmured to the couple.

"*Denke*, Leila." Ada patted her hand. "*Gott* will provide. Our friends will help us build again. We didn't have anything that can't be replaced. Our *kinder* are alive, and so are you. That is what matters."

"How did you get out?" Jonah wondered. His face was pale, but he didn't seem to be upset with them.

"Remember the tour you gave me? You showed me the attic."

"You escaped by climbing on the tree."

Leila shuddered. "It was a harrowing experience, to be sure. But if you hadn't shown him that, we never would have escaped. So I guess you can say that you saved our lives."

Jonah seemed to like that idea.

The driver called out for them to hurry. Leila grabbed Evie's stuff and loaded the booster seat into the car. She buckled her daughter in and thanked the Weavers before getting in beside her daughter. Katie hugged her parents and her brother and hopped into the back seat so that she and Leila were on either side of Evie like bookends.

Brett had one last piece of advice to give the Weavers. "If you have anywhere else to stay for a few days—"

"We will stay with family. Don't worry about us," David informed him.

He'd done all he could for them. Brett got into the front seat next to their grumpy driver. Ignoring the man's astonished look, he pulled out his phone and sent a text update to the chief. She texted back almost immediately.

Glad you are all safe. The department will pay for anything the family might need. They won't have to pay anything out of pocket.

Satisfied, he put his phone away. He'd expected that response.

The chief would expect him to contact her at regular intervals. He had no idea if there was electricity in Katie's cousin's barn like there had been in her dad's. The difference was that her dad ran his business out of their barn. If there wasn't electricity at their new location, he would have to come up with a different plan.

He couldn't be out of communication for days at a time. Not with an active murder investigation going on and a killer on a rampage.

He'd have to wait until they arrived in New Wilmington before he asked Katie. He didn't want to talk about police business in front of an outsider.

Apparently, the driver had worked as a tour guide once near New Wilmington. Once he discovered that neither

Brett nor Leila had visited the area, his grouchy demeanor changed. Suddenly, he was excited to give them the true flavor of the area.

"New Wilmington is the third-largest Amish community in Pennsylvania," he informed them as they neared the area. "See those buggies?"

Brett noted the burnt-orange buggies.

"This is the only place in the country where the buggies are that color," the driver said proudly.

Brett glanced over his shoulder in time to see Katie roll her eyes at Leila. He wiped his mouth to smother the grin that threatened to spread across his face. While he appreciated the driver's enthusiasm, it was amusing, especially considering his attitude at the beginning of their journey.

He did enjoy seeing the Banks Bridge, a white covered bridge that was, according to the young man, famous for being in an episode of a television show years ago. As Brett's family hadn't had a television after his dad had destroyed theirs in a drunken rage, he hadn't seen most shows.

He still didn't own a television, a fact most people who knew him found mind-boggling. He could not bring himself to waste the money to buy one. Besides, from hearing his coworkers talk, it seemed all they showed were cop shows and crime dramas. He spent all day dealing with people who broke the law. While he loved his job, there were times when seeing the level of depravity people were capable of depressed him.

He didn't need to see more of it in his home.

It was after lunch when they finally arrived at the home of Vera Weaver. Brett paid the driver, even though Katie protested, and helped unload the luggage. Vera stood on the front porch, waving.

She was younger than Brett had imagined. He didn't

know of any young Amish women who lived in houses by themselves. Most of them lived with family.

"Vera was an only *kind*," Katie had informed them. "Both her parents were killed in an accident years ago when a car full of college students ran a red light and plowed into their buggy."

Gazing at the slender young woman standing on the porch, he sympathized. She was in her early twenties and should have been married and raising a family. When she walked, it was with a definite limp. Katie had told them she'd been in the buggy with her parents. Her leg had been crushed. It had taken her a year to learn how to walk again.

None of that showed on her face. Her mouth stretched wide in a happy smile, and her blue eyes gleamed with good humor. "Katie! It is *gut* to see you! *Cumme!* Bring your friends inside. I have lunch on the table."

"How did she know we were coming?" Leila asked. "I thought she didn't have a phone."

"She runs a business. That building behind the barn is her store. She sells crafts, food she cans and preserves, baked goods. Since she has a business, she is allowed to have electricity and a phone there," Katie murmured. "I called her during her work hours to let her know we would *cumme* and see her."

"Does she know?" Brett asked. He didn't specify what. She'd figure it out.

"Some. Enough to know why this is necessary. You can tell her the rest. I wasn't sure how much I should say."

Brett nodded but didn't comment until the driver had returned to his vehicle and started backing out of the driveway.

"Vera." Katie embraced her cousin. "I want you to meet my friends. First, the most important." She put a hand on Evie's shoulder. "This is Evelyn. We call her Evie."

Evie giggled, pleased to be introduced first.

Then Katie introduced Brett and Leila.

"Well, *cumme. Cumme.* We can eat. Then you can tell me the story."

When he entered the house, the scent of fresh bread overwhelmed him. His mouth began to water. Next to him, Leila's stomach grumbled.

"I guess it's time to eat," she said without a trace of embarrassment.

"*Ja!* I have plenty."

A few minutes later, Brett saw she meant what she said. There was enough food to feed an army. They all tucked in. For the first few minutes, no one talked.

When lunch ended, Vera showed them all to their rooms. A tiny cot had been set up in Leila's room for Evie. It was earlier than normal for her nap, but the child climbed into the bed and tucked her unicorn under her chin. She fell asleep quickly.

Brett's mouth fell open.

Leila laughed softly. "I expected that. Car trips wear her out. Tomorrow, she'll be back to her normal energetic self."

His heart melted when she placed a gentle kiss on her daughter's head. Leila was a good mom. A strong mom who did her best to put her daughter first.

He hadn't had that. How would his life have been different if he'd had a parent like her? Well, it hadn't happened, so it was better not to dwell on it.

After stowing his bags in the room Vera led him to, he checked to make sure his gun was safely hidden under his shirt. He knew Leila had her phone in her pocket.

That reminded him.

"Vera. I was wondering if we'd be able to charge our

phones in your office. I need to be able to check in with my chief daily."

"*Ja.* I have electricity there."

Next to him, Leila expelled a large sigh of relief. He grinned down at her and winked. She scrunched her nose back at him.

He had to admit, he always wanted to tap the end of her nose when she gave him that look. Or kiss her. But neither would be appropriate.

Vera led the way back to the kitchen. She poured coffee into large mugs and put them on the table.

"Now that Evie is asleep, you can tell me why you are here."

He took a sip of the coffee. He'd gotten used to drinking it black, but this coffee was very strong. He'd be tempted to put cream in it if there had been some on the table.

Setting his mug down again, he took a breath to prepare himself and began to tell the story.

Leila listened to Brett talk. She was impressed. He took the important details and told them clearly and concisely. He didn't diminish the horror of the past few days or of the killer's crimes, but he also didn't embellish. Every word was textbook precise.

She couldn't have told the story. Not without becoming emotional. It had been a challenge to tell the other cops at the police station. The first attack had still been fresh on her mind. But at that time she had no idea how fast the situation would go downhill. Every time she thought of what she'd been through in the past three days, she was amazed that she hadn't collapsed into a heap, crying in the middle of the floor.

Until her sister died, Leila hadn't really believed people went through such things. Now, she knew fairy tales weren't real, but she still struggled to comprehend that anyone could treat another so horribly.

Vera listened to the story without speaking. Leila waited for the moment when she would see Vera decide that no, they couldn't stay with her. It never happened. Not even when she heard about Katie's house being set on fire.

"*Ach.* You've been through so much. But you're here now, ain't so? Rest up today. You have earned it."

Leila briefly wondered how Vera would run her store if she stayed with them in the house. Her question was answered when the first buggy drove into the parking lot. When the two women got down from the buggy and headed to the store, she heard a bell ring. Vera calmly set her coffee down and walked across to the store. She was gone for about twenty minutes. After her customers left, she returned to the house. She had to leave half a dozen times during the course of the afternoon to tend to her shop.

While she was gone, Katie took it upon herself to fix the evening's supper. Leila offered to help and was roundly denied.

"*Nee.* Vera said you should rest today. Tomorrow you can help. Thursdays are busy days at her store. Maybe we'll walk over and you can see it in action."

She agreed, but she didn't know that she'd want to leave the safety of the house for that long. Letting other people know she was here seemed counterintuitive. They were supposed to be hiding out. What good did it do to hide if everyone knew she was here?

Although, with her Amish clothes, she was disguised.

After dinner, she went to sit on the front porch swing to think. The door squeaked open behind her. Soon, the swing dipped with Brett's weight.

"Brett," she asked him. "Do you think the killer saw me dressed Amish? At the Weaver house?"

He took a swig of his water before answering. "I wondered about that. I've decided probably not. When he shot at me, you were already pretty hidden on the roof of the barn. He never took a shot at you. If he had seen you, he would have tried to get to you."

"I keep expecting him to show up any moment."

They sat silently. When his hand came to rest on top of hers, it startled her for a moment. She nearly yanked her hand away. But she didn't. The feel of his hand comforted her in a way she hadn't felt in a long time. But it was more than that.

Her pulse sped up. She turned her head away from him, sure that her cheeks were on fire. No man had affected her like this in so long. She didn't know what to do with these feelings. Or if she should just ignore them.

She was not in a position to indulge in a relationship. She recalled Brett's story. For him to get emotionally involved with anyone after what he'd been through would take guts. She had seen her sister's body. And she'd seen murder victims. But she'd never held one in her arms as they died. Especially not someone she loved.

Brett's phone rang, jerking her from her thoughts.

"Chief?" As he listened, Leila could hear the woman's voice, although she couldn't make out the words. Beside her, Brett's body tightened. She felt the energy, the anger, coming from him in waves.

Something told her that the chief's call was about her and that he was angry on her behalf. He hung up soon after.

"Well?" If it was about her, she had a right to know.

"Our killer hasn't given up on you. A man, wearing dark glasses with a mustache and a beard, has been seen showing your picture around near Katie's house. One of the neighbors thought the beard and mustache were fake. Apparently, he hasn't figured out that you've come out here."

Her breath came faster. "Did anyone identify me, do you think?"

"No. No one knew who you were. And when you left, even if they saw you, they would have seen an Amish woman with Katie. Trust me, when I first saw you dressed in Amish clothes, it threw me for a loop. Took me a minute to realize it was you."

She flushed. That was when she'd run to him and hugged him on the driveway. The memory was still fresh in her mind.

He must have remembered it, too. He turned his face away.

Then a giggle struck her. His head whipped toward her.

"I'm imaging your face when some strange Amish woman ran and hugged you."

He laughed. "It shocked me. I'm not gonna lie."

Their laughter died. They had somehow moved closer together in the last few moments. Their eyes met.

"Leila."

She saw it in his eyes. He was going to kiss her. Did she want him to? His face came closer and she closed her eyes.

The door banged open. "Mommy, I can't go to sleep. I'm scared."

Leila jumped off the swing so fast she nearly tipped it over. Refusing to look at Brett, she rushed to her daughter. "Come on, sweetie. I'll sing you to sleep, like we do at home."

She'd almost kissed him. What had she been thinking? She couldn't decide if she was happy that Evie had interrupted them or not. But she knew it couldn't happen again.

* * *

Brett dropped his face in his hands and groaned. What had happened? Since when did he go around kissing women? Never! He wasn't one for casual relationships. And hadn't he already decided that she was off-limits until they got this situation under control?

Apparently, all it took was a quiet moment and being alone with her for all his good intentions to flee. He was mortified. Embarrassed. Angry with himself.

And disappointed that Evie had interrupted them.

Maybe that had been providence, as well. He didn't know yet if he wanted to pursue Leila. They both had so many issues. But even if he did want to, he didn't know how she'd feel about it.

But when he'd moved in to kiss her, she hadn't backed away. He would not soon forget the way her eyes had deepened before her lids fluttered closed. If Evie hadn't come out, she would have let him kiss her.

And that would have been disastrous. How would they face each other the next day?

It was going to be embarrassing to see her, but at least they'd stopped before it went too far.

He needed to do something.

Standing, he made sure his Glock was secure at his back. He left the porch and made a full sweep around the house. Finding no threats, he widened his sweep to include the shop and the surrounding land. He needed to stay on top of what was happening.

He'd not said it when they were talking, but he did worry about someone giving away Katie's relationship to Vera. Not maliciously. But if the killer was skulking around, would he overhear something that led him out here? He needed to keep a close eye.

Reaching for his phone, he dialed the chief back.

"Lieutenant."

"Chief. I was thinking, you might want to have someone watching out for the Weaver family. If our guy's waiting around, trying to find out where she is—"

"I'm already on it, Brett. Don't you worry about it. I have contacted the precincts in the area. They are all aware of the situation. We're being very proactive with this case."

There was nothing more to be said.

But he couldn't stop the thoughts going around and around in his mind. All it would take was one small mistake and he could lose her.

Even if she never became more than a friend to him, Leila Britton was a precious part of his life, at least as long as she allowed him in it. But even if she decided tomorrow that she wanted nothing to do with him, he'd sleep better knowing that she was in the world, safe.

He walked back into the house. The night was coming on fast, and soon everyone would be sleeping.

He wasn't sure if he'd be able to rest, knowing a killer was out there, searching for Leila.

To ensure Leila and her daughter remained unharmed, Brett vowed to do whatever he needed to.

No matter what price he had to pay.

THIRTEEN

A day later, Brett shut the door behind him, taking care that it didn't bang and wake Evie from her nap. He walked down the steps and out to the pasture. He didn't want the rest of the house's occupants overhearing police business. Chief Kaiser's text seemed to imply something serious had happened. He had a bad feeling about it.

He didn't need to be an expert to know something significant had occurred. Otherwise, she would have waited for him to call in.

He dialed her direct number. She picked up immediately. "Thanks for getting back to me, Lieutenant."

"Sure, Chief. Your text sounded urgent."

"It is. Our killer has struck again."

For a second, it felt like a punch in the gut. The feeling was so intense, Brett bent over, hands on his knees. When he felt like he could take a full breath again, he straightened.

"Who was it? And where was her body found?" Should he get Leila out of here? Questions pummeled him, but when the chief started talking again, he tuned in.

"We've caught a break with this one. The victim got away. The woman is Hillary Gavens, age twenty-three. Our killer tried to grab Miss Gavens while she was on her morning run. He came up behind her near the park on Myrtle

Drive. He tried dragging her toward the old pavilion there, you know, the one with three closed sides?"

"Yeah. I know the one. What do mean by he *tried* to drag her into it?"

"Miss Gavens has been watching the news. She saw that there have been several women with her coloring murdered. She took precautions and had her dog running with her. I don't approve of letting your dog go without a leash, but in this case, I'm giving her the benefit of the doubt. Her dog, a large retriever and shepherd mix, was exploring. When our guy attacked her, he came running and nearly took the killer's arm off. The killer escaped."

"Did she see his face?"

"No, but I'm hoping there's something about him she'll remember. She didn't when Officer Witt took her statement earlier, but maybe after she has time to calm down, something will come to mind."

"Was she injured?" She had survived. Leila would be glad to hear that.

"No. She was shaken up, obviously. And she twisted her ankle when he tried to drag her. Other than that, she's unharmed. The ambulance took her to the ER just to be sure. And they've already set her up with a therapist."

"She'll probably have nightmares from this." That wouldn't be fun to deal with, but again, she had her life. He praised God for that.

"Listen, we're working on a lead here. I'll keep you in the loop. If you don't hear from me, call in at the regular time."

"Will do, Chief. Thanks for the update." He hung up the phone and wandered back toward the house. Katie, Vera and Leila were laughing about something in the living room. When he walked in, they had quilting projects scattered around the room. "Everything okay here, ladies?"

"Yes," Leila said, rolling her eyes at her friends. "They were showing me some of their epic failures from when they were first learning to quilt."

He smiled. Instead of smiling back, Leila's eyes grew serious. She walked over and took his hand, surprising him.

"You look like you've had bad news. Care to share?"

She read him so well. He didn't have to say a word and she understood his mood. "I just talked to the chief."

"Oh. Okay." She turned to address Vera and Katie. "I need to talk with Brett privately. I will be back."

"Take your time," Katie said. Vera just waved them away.

Brett tightened his fingers on Leila's hand. "Let's go outside."

When they got outside, he still had her hand in his. He told himself to let it go, but his body refused to follow his mind's instructions.

"Brett, what is it? What's happened?"

He faced her. "The chief wanted me to know that another woman was attacked."

She gasped, her free hand flying to cover her mouth. "Oh, no!"

"But this time, she escaped." He went on to give her all the details.

"I'm so glad that she got away!" Leila exclaimed. "But I wonder how he'll react."

"Yeah. I know. I wondered, too."

She chewed her lower lip. "It's been two days since we came here. Two days without incident. I'm not ready to let down my guard, not by any means, but I find myself hopeful that he won't find me here. With this new development, I hope it means that he's beginning to make mistakes."

"Yeah. Because if he is, it might lead to his downfall."

It couldn't happen soon enough. Brett was ready for the

killer to be caught so he could see the fear leave Leila's beautiful brown eyes.

Although he wasn't looking forward to the day when he had to try and move forward without her. He wasn't even sure if he could. At least, not while they worked so close together.

He thought she might have some feelings for him, too. He'd seen her watching him, caught her blushing when they touched accidentally. Was there a way for them to be together and find out if they could be a couple for good?

One thing for sure: It wasn't a possibility while she was running for her life. And afterward, they'd have to work through their emotional issues.

If she was interested.

If she wasn't, somehow he'd have to find a way to let her go.

Leila shook her head, astonished at what Brett had told her. The woman TBK had singled out to be victim number eight had gotten away. She worried he might try to go after the woman again. However, knowing she had that fierce canine protector, maybe he'd count his losses and move on.

How long until he tried to kill again?

In less than a week, he'd slain one woman and tried to kill another. That was different from before, when his crimes were spaced out by a year or so. She shuddered.

Brett still had a hold on her hand. She should let it go and walk away. But she couldn't. Not yet. Hearing about the latest attack left her feeling raw. His hold on her soothed some of the edge away.

When she caught the direction her thoughts were flowing, she gently removed her hand from his. The flash of hurt in his eyes made her regret the move instantly. She didn't want to hurt him. But didn't he realize she wasn't good for him?

She had too many issues. There was no room in her life for romance.

Her heart tried to argue that her daughter needed a father.

But she'd been without one for most of her life. She had no memories of Will. She'd only been a baby when he'd died.

Leila thought about her own childhood. She'd had her mom and Tara, but her father had played the biggest role in her life. She'd always been her daddy's girl, much more so than Tara. While Tara was the one who wanted to bake cookies and work in the garden with their mother, Leila had trotted after their dad, helping on the cars or hiding away in his office to discuss books they'd read.

She missed her father, she realized.

When he'd remarried, she'd been surprised to receive an invitation. She hadn't known he'd met anyone. She hadn't given the woman, Kelly, a chance. Had she even responded to the invitation?

Maybe she would have relented and reached out to him at some point, but then Will had betrayed her and died. That had wrecked her emotionally. To the point she'd squashed any idea of reconciling with her father.

She'd rejected her father when he'd tried to reach out to her and invite her back into his life.

The truth shocked her.

For years, she'd blamed him for abandoning her. And maybe he had, for a while. But she had abandoned him, too. She'd lost her twin and her mother, but he'd lost his wife and his daughter. Why hadn't she considered his grief?

She'd never realized how selfish her decisions had been.

Her father didn't even know his granddaughter. Not really. He'd seen her a few times, but they'd been strangers for so long. And then she moved back to Pennsylvania. Had she even told him she was moving across the country?

She didn't think she had. She had completely shut him out of her life.

"Leila?"

She lifted her face and saw Brett through a blurry veil of tears. "Oh, Brett. I just realized something awful about myself."

The tears slipped down her face as she related to him her discovery.

He groaned. "Oh, honey. I'm so sorry."

When his arms wrapped around her, she allowed herself to lean against him and accept his comfort. But only for a moment. If she allowed herself to cry, she feared she'd never stop. She put her hand on his chest to create some distance between them. Instead, feeling the solid thump of his heartbeat under her hand and the intimacy of their posture increased, regardless of the greater space between them.

He bent and lightly kissed her forehead.

Her entire face flushed. What would happen if he kissed her for real?

Stop! She couldn't let this continue. Letting out a shaky laugh, she backed away. His arms dropped away from her. "We're in front of an Amish woman's home. This is hardly appropriate."

Brett barked out a surprised laugh. "I hadn't thought of it that way."

"I need to go get myself together. Evie will be waking up soon. When she does, I don't want to be an emotional mess."

"Listen, if the chief calls and I hear anything more, I'll

let you know. Even though you're in hiding, and I'm your bodyguard for the moment, you are still part of our team. I don't want you to feel like we're treating you like a princess in a tower."

She raised her eyebrows. "Me, a princess? Hardly."

She made her getaway a moment later, returning to the house. When she walked in, she heard Katie calling her name. Calling herself a coward, she didn't acknowledge the call but hurried up the stairs to the room she shared with her daughter. She grabbed her phone and sat on her bed. She looked over at her sleeping daughter on the little cot. It comforted her to be in the room with her.

When this was over, she'd contact her father, she promised herself. It was possible that he'd reject her, not wanting to risk that pain again. But somehow she doubted it. Her eyes hovered on the sleeping child. She didn't think Evie could ever do anything that would make her want to completely dissolve ties with her.

Someday, she prayed, her little girl would grow up and move on with her own life. Maybe marry and have children of her own.

She wanted to be part of that, as much as it would hurt to see her moving on. It was part of life.

She brought up her dad's contact information. Was he still at that same number?

She could call him now. Or send him a text.

She set her phone down, chickening out. What could she tell him? *Hey, Dad, I'm on the run from Tara's killer.*

No. She couldn't put him through that. Not again. If the unthinkable happened, he'd be less hurt if they never reconnected. But if they put TBK behind bars, she'd reach out to her dad. She'd take that risk, so that Evie could have a grandparent in her life. Will's parents hadn't been interested in remaining in contact after their son had died.

There wasn't any hurt she wouldn't risk for the sake of her daughter.

Picking up her phone again, she opened the Bible app she'd downloaded. It had been so long since she'd read the Bible. She didn't own one anymore. Shame filled her. A long time ago, her parents had given her one, but in a moment of rage, she'd gotten rid of it.

She bent her head and whispered her repentance to God. She'd turned her back on her dad and Him. A sense of peace filled her heart. She knew that God would take her back into His fold. Whether or not the humans surrounding her lived up to her expectations didn't matter. God always would.

Closing her eyes, she fell into a healing sleep.

A small hand on her face woke her. Evie giggled at her. "You were snoring, Mommy."

Leila laughed. "I was waiting for my kiddo to wake up and I fell asleep. Why don't we go downstairs and see what Katie is doing?"

"Yay!"

Evie bounced off the bed and skipped to the door, ready to see Katie. Slipping off the bed, Leila put her phone in her pocket. Her hands touched her watch. She really didn't need both items. She shrugged. It didn't hurt. She didn't want to lose her watch. Keeping it in her pocket seemed innocent enough. It didn't take up much space.

She followed Evie downstairs into the kitchen. Katie and Vera were talking and laughing together, their voices comforting. When she entered with Evie, they broke off their conversation.

Katie walked over to her. "Is all *gut*?"

Immediately she regretted ignoring her earlier. "Yes. Sorry. I went to check on Evie and ended up falling asleep."

"I understand. Vera wants to start canning tomatoes after lunch. Do you want to help?"

"I've never done it before. Will I be in the way?"

"Nee." Vera stirred something in the pot on the stove. "Canning is easier with many hands."

"It's a long process," Katie agreed.

"I might just do that." She didn't want to commit herself, just in case she really did get in the way. She'd never been into tasks like gardening and canning. But she did enjoy spending time with these women. Katie and Vera looked at life so simply, and their strong faith amazed her. She wanted to have faith like that. The kind that defined her whole life and directed every decision.

Brett wandered in at lunchtime. They sat together for a simple meal of chicken salad on homemade Amish croissants, otherwise known as Amish Butterhorn rolls, assorted cut-up fruit, potato chips and sliced cucumber.

"The best meals are those where you can take what you have on hand and just put it on the table," Vera informed them.

She had a point. Their fare wasn't fancy, and it didn't take a lot of preparation, but she enjoyed it immensely. The buttery rolls were flaky and melted in her mouth Evie hadn't been too sure about the chicken salad, but she ate it. Leila had never eaten chicken salad with cranberries and walnuts before, and she said so.

"Is this an old family recipe?"

Vera shook her head. "I had some leftover chicken I needed to use. I decided to throw in the cranberries and walnuts to see if they worked. I guess they did."

"I'd agree."

The lunch dishes had just been put away when a Sterling Ridge Police Department cruiser pulled into the driveway.

"That's Carter." Brett shoved his feet into his boots. "I didn't expect to see him here. I better go and check on what he wants."

She watched him leave, her heart pounding. To bring him here, it had to be either really good news…or really bad.

"Carter! I didn't expect to see you here. I just talked with the chief a few hours ago."

Carter shut the car door behind him. "I know you did. But there have been some interesting developments since then."

Brett braced himself. "Tell me."

"We have a suspect in custody, and I like him for the murders."

The breath whooshed out of Brett. Could it be over this quickly?

"Who? Don't leave me hanging here!"

"Shane Kelso."

"Why do I know that name?" He couldn't quite place it.

"He works at the same lab that Leila is contracted through."

"Yeah." He could see him now. "He helped us carry her camera equipment out the other day."

"Uh-huh. He would know when she was back in town, where her precincts were and even what cases she would take."

"I can see that. So how did you figure out it was him?"

"The van that had been stolen, the one he'd driven for a couple of days? It was found abandoned this morning. The team is still sweeping it for any evidence. He'd wiped it pretty clean, except he dropped a business card with his name on it under the seat. When we brought up his image and matched it with the traffic cams we found this..."

Carter brought up a video on his phone. The image was grainy. But the man sitting behind the steering wheel of the van at a traffic light could have been Shane. The top of his face was hidden by a baseball cap, but the jaw, the hair...

"It looks like the guy who helped us."

Carter put his phone back in his pocket. "Yeah. Not a perfect image. There's enough blurriness that a juror could say they don't think it's the same person. So the chief wants to bring in the victim and see if she can ID him. We all doubt it. She couldn't have seen his face. When he attacked Leila, he always wore a Grim Reaper mask. This newest victim remembers some kind of mask. But maybe his stature or something. And we have a warrant to search his place."

That was something. If it turned out to be Shane, then Leila was safe, and she and Evie could return home.

At the thought, an emptiness opened up inside him.

Because that would mean their time together would be over.

But he refused to be selfish. Leila needed closure and that child needed to go back to her carefree innocence. He'd pay the price of his broken heart to make that happen. But maybe, one day, once she recovered and was ready to move on, they could be together.

Because Brett knew without a doubt that he was head over heels for Leila Britton, and he didn't see that changing, ever.

FOURTEEN

"What did Carter want?" Leila asked, snatching a strawberry off a fruit platter and popping it into her mouth. The berries were sweet and juicy. She grabbed another one and bit into it.

Brett looked at her. "He has some news, but I'm going to let him share it. We were on our way in when Joe called him. So he'll have more details than what he just told me."

Leila considered herself a patient person, but this was more than she could stand. Was it good news or bad news? Brett didn't look angry or stern. Actually, she couldn't decipher his mood at all. She tapped her foot on the floor. She hated waiting. Five minutes later, Carter called her and Brett back outside.

"It's official. The killer is in custody." He clapped his hands together.

She gasped. "Really?"

"Yep. I'm sure you're familiar with the name Shane Kelso," Carter said to her.

She nearly fell over in shock. She could barely process what he'd said.

"Wait. You can't be serious. Shane is the killer?" Leila blurted. "Shane that I worked with?"

She pictured the sweet man who was always available

to help out. He had even seemed shy at times. Granted, she didn't know that much about him, but there was nothing about him that had ever seemed dangerous. In fact, sometimes he looked so sad with his puppy-dog eyes.

But the police wouldn't have arrested him without evidence.

Carter's look was kind and sympathetic, as if he understood the pain she felt from knowing someone she worked with was a killer. "It's hard to believe, I know, but we're confident it was him. Ryan and Joe have gone to arrest him and bring him in. The chief wanted me to come and tell you two that your vacation is over and it is time to return to work."

Brett scoffed. "Vacation? You do know that we've been on the run from Shane for the past few days. How did he find us at Katie's, by the way?"

"We don't know that yet. All I know is that it's safe for Leila to return home."

Leila couldn't wrap her mind around this turn of events. Shane Kelso had murdered her sister. He had tried to murder her.

The worst one to imagine, though, was him walking into an elderly woman's house and shooting her at close range.

"I don't know," she said, shaking her head. "It's not that I doubt you, but this is hard to accept. I feel like we're missing something."

Brett placed an arm on her back. She leaned into him, accepting the comfort and warmth he offered. She was so cold inside. She wrapped her arms around her middle to keep from shaking.

"Why did he pick Leila in the first place?" Brett asked. His voice had a rough edge to it. She had sensed his deepening feelings for her. Knowing they had the person in custody would affect him, too.

Carter glanced between them. "It seems that Leila did know Shane before. They attended college together."

"We did? I don't remember that." Mentally, she ran through the people she'd hung out with at college. Shane wasn't someone she recalled.

"Yep. When we checked into it, it seems you had several classes together. When we searched his apartment this morning, we found some incriminating news clippings and photos. Apparently, he's been stalking you for a decade."

A shudder went down her spine. She had never had any idea until now that someone had been watching her. Her gut churned.

"What now?" she asked.

"Hillary Gavens is coming in to see him in a lineup. I doubt she'll be able to pick him out. He was wearing a mask," Carter answered.

Leila nodded. "Yeah. I don't know how she'd be able to identify him."

She remembered the Grim Reaper mask he wore. She would see it in her nightmares for years to come, if not for the rest of her life. While she was still shocked that someone like Shane could be a murderer, she would be forever grateful that he'd been caught before he did any more harm.

Brett rubbed her shoulder as he continued speaking. "Carter and I need to conference with the chief. I think it would be best if we don't set up our Wi-Fi inside the Weaver house."

For the first time since this conversation started, she smiled.

"Probably not. Katie has already stuck her neck out for

us enough as it is. Plus, I really don't want Evie to hear this conversation."

Carter thought for a moment. "I think I know what we can do. There's a little restaurant in town with a private back room. If we tell them we need it for police business, I'm sure they will let us have it for an hour or two."

A knot formed in the pit of her stomach. On the one hand, she understood they believed the danger was over. But she still felt antsy. And now Carter and Brett were heading into town. They were leaving her here. She wished she owned a gun. Next chance she got, she would apply for a concealed-carry permit. But for now, she was going to be here, alone, without protection.

She would be fine, she admonished herself. It they'd caught TBK, it meant she didn't need protection. The force behind the terror was in jail and couldn't touch her, or anyone else. Why didn't she feel comforted? Maybe she wouldn't feel like it was real until she returned home and saw for herself that he was gone.

She always had been one that needed to see the proof before she had believed something. Maybe that was why it had taken so long for her to turn back to God. She needed Him now, more than ever.

Brett was watching her with concern. She needed to be strong. He would worry if she couldn't get her act together and act like she could handle this. She couldn't interfere with his work. He was too important to her. She gave him what she hoped was a confident smile.

He searched her face for a moment before the corners of his mouth tipped up. Good. That was the look she wanted.

"I guess I'll feed Evie and then start getting our things together for the trip back to Sterling Ridge."

Brett narrowed his eyes at her. "You're still worried. If

it would help, I am sure you can stay at Michaela's again tonight."

Her face heated. "No. That won't be necessary. I'm just a bit wary. It feels—I don't know—staged."

He stilled. "I can stay here if—"

She shook herself from her strange mood and forced a smile on her face. "No, go with Lieutenant Flint. I'm sure I'm overthinking this. Just because the Brand Killer was found easier than I expected doesn't mean a mistake was made."

Carter urged Brett to hurry, but Brett clearly didn't want to leave her. She should have kept her worries to herself. She was keeping him from his duty, and for what? If they had caught the killer, then she needed to get used to not having him around at all times.

That thought bothered her more than it should.

But why?

She had been alone for a long time. After William, she had decided there was no place for a man in her life. But these past few days with Brett had opened her mind to what a true partnership with a man could be.

Did she have feelings for Brett?

Uncomfortably, she squirmed. She didn't care for the questions her self-reflection had conjured up.

"I'll be back soon," Brett assured her. "We can head back home as soon as I return."

"Sure. Don't worry about me. I'll keep busy. It will be nice to get back."

He gave her a look that clearly said he didn't believe her but let it go.

"Hey, Carter!"

Carter turned back, his hand falling from the cruiser door handle. "Yeah?"

"Give me five. I want to change back into uniform since we'll be on official business."

"I'll wait here."

Brett brushed past her and went swiftly to his room. When he emerged a few minutes later, her pulse sped up. She couldn't remember seeing anything as handsome as Brett in his uniform. He kissed her cheek so quickly she could have dreamed it. Then he followed his colleague to the cruiser.

Leila stood on the porch and watched Brett and Carter pull away. Brett's warm gaze collided with hers and she felt a strange fluttering in her stomach.

She could no longer deny that something about the honest police lieutenant spoke to her soul and touched her heart. What she didn't know was what she was going to do with that knowledge—or if these feelings were even real. She'd heard of stressful situations making people believe they were falling in love when it was just the intensity of the situation.

Still, she wondered. Did he have any thoughts about her? When she realized she was wondering what it would feel like to kiss him or to be held in his arms, she pulled herself back from those thoughts.

Enough. This is nonsense. I'm a grown woman with a child to raise. I cannot let myself forget that.

She turned her back on the retreating cruiser and reentered the house. In the kitchen, she found Katie and Evie baking cookies.

"Mommy, look!" Evie said, her face smeared with chocolate. "Me and Katie are making chocolate chip cookies. Yummy!"

She smiled at her daughter. "Those are my favorite."

Katie laughed. "And if Evie stops eating the cookies, maybe we'll even have some left for you."

"Well, I have some interesting news to share," she told Katie quietly. "Apparently, the person the police have been looking for has been caught. So Evie and I—we'll be going back to Sterling Ridge this afternoon."

Katie's mouth fell open in a round O. She glanced down at Evie, then back at Leila. "That was quick, ain't so?"

"Yeah, it was quick."

A little too quick. No, no, no. She needed to stop doubting and just be grateful that they had caught the man who had killed her sister—and who wanted to kill her as well.

"Would you be okay watching Evie a little longer while I go and pack our things?"

"Of course."

Leila looked around. "I thought you were helping your cousin can today."

Katie spooned another round ball of dough onto the cookie sheet. "She needed something and decided to head to the store. She'll be back soon. It's just down the road. I'm not worried."

Leila could not imagine being that casual in the current situation, but then Katie knew her cousin best. She was a guest here.

She walked down the hallway to her room to collect the bags and start packing. When she passed Vera's room, she heard a scuffling noise. That was strange. Katie had said Vera had gone to the store.

She knocked on the door. "Vera?" she called softly. "Are you all right?"

The scuffling stopped. A loud groan answered her.

Concerned that Vera might be sick, Leila pushed the door open and stepped into the room.

Vera's terrified eyes stared at her. The woman sat in the rocking chair, duct tape over her mouth, a thick rope wrapped around her, tying her to the chair. She gave Leila a fierce head shake.

Spinning around, Leila tried to scream.

The man—the man in the mask standing against the wall—rushed forward and grabbed her, his hand over her mouth.

"You don't want to do that. There are too many vulnerable people in this house. I've already killed seven people. I have no problem killing three more."

He'd kill Evie. And Katie and Vera. She had no choice but to keep silent.

She'd been right. Shane hadn't been the killer. And now the real TBK had found her.

Brett and Carter entered the restaurant. The lunch rush was in full swing. The hostess greeted them with a smile, swiping the counter with rag.

"Y'all can sit wherever you like," she called out. "Pippa will be over in a minute to get your drinks."

"Actually, we wanted to set up in your back room, if it wouldn't be a problem. We have police business and need to do an online meeting."

She quirked an eyebrow at him. "Well, that shouldn't be an issue, since it's not reserved. Let me check."

She dropped her rag in a bucket behind the counter and flittered through a swinging door. Brett heard the murmur of voices for a minute before she returned. "It's not a problem. We can even pull the pocket door shut. Just make sure you're out of there before three."

It was going on one in the afternoon now.

"We'll be done before that," Brett assured her. "We appreciate it."

"Pippa!"

A young waitress with bright red curls sauntered over. "Yes, Grace?"

"Please take these officers to the back room, see that they have what they need, then close the pocket door."

"Will do." She gave them a bright smile. "Follow me, please."

Within five minutes, they were seated and Carter was working on connecting the computer to his hot spot. Pippa came over to bring each man an ice-cold glass of Pepsi and a slice of pepperoni pizza.

"If you need anything else, go ahead and ding the bell." She put the bell in question on the table. "Otherwise, I'll leave you alone so you can have your privacy."

"Perfect." Carter smiled at her.

She whisked the empty tray off the table and marched out, pulling the door closed as she exited.

"Okay, the Wi-Fi is set up." Carter turned the computer so they could both see it and started the meeting. He sent the chief an invitation. Within a minute, Chief Kaiser joined them.

"Gentlemen, we have some new updates for you."

Her serious tone got Brett's attention immediately. This was not the face of a chief celebrating the capture of a notorious serial killer.

"Ma'am?"

"Our witness, the woman TBK attacked yesterday, came in today. We had Shane Kelso in a lineup. I honestly thought she wouldn't identify anyone, since her attacker was masked, and so I wasn't surprised when she said she didn't see him. But then she asked them all to hold out their left hands, so she could see them."

Both Carter and Brett straightened in their seats.

"Why?" Brett asked, urgency flooding his body. He'd left Leila, even though she'd thought something felt off. Right now he had a feeling he should have trusted his gut and stayed with her.

"When she fought her assailant, one of his gloves came off," the chief replied. "She said his hand looked like it had third-degree burns covering it. Shane's hands had no such markings. And there's more." She paused, then continued. "The pictures Shane had weren't of Leila."

Brett caught on immediately. "Tara?"

She nodded. "He'd met Tara when she'd visited her sister on campus. The two of them dated secretly for a while. She was trying to get into acting. He didn't think his family would approve of her because of their views on actors and people in the arts in general."

Brett felt like the air had been sucked out of the room. "Did you corroborate his story?"

"Doing that now, but I think we'll be releasing him within the next couple of hours. We don't have enough evidence to keep him." Her voice deepened as she continued. "When we told Shane that we wanted to see if he had burn scars on his hands, he said that it wasn't him. His older brother, who had also gone to school with him, had been in a fire and had scars on his hands. His name is Xavier Kelso. We're waiting on a warrant to search his house right now."

His chest pounding, Brett stood. "Chief, we have to go. We left Leila unprotected."

"You two go. I'll let you know when I have news."

Carter shut the computer. "I'm sure she's fine."

Brett didn't respond. He tried to call her. When her

phone went to voicemail, his muscles tightened. Until he saw Leila in person, no words would soothe the fire burning in his gut. She might be in danger even now. He jogged out to the cruiser, anxious to see her.

Carter paid the bill and came after him. They made the journey quietly. When they got back to the house, Brett hopped out and started to run toward the porch. A shiny object on the gravel caught his attention. Bending down, he picked up Leila's phone. It was shattered, as if a car had run over it.

Now he knew something was wrong.

He didn't even knock. He charged into the house, Carter close on his heels. Evie's sobs hit his ears. He ran into the kitchen and found her with Katie and Vera at the table.

"Brett!" Evie shrieked, then threw herself into his arms.

"Evie, what's wrong?" He turned to Katie. "Where's Leila?"

Vera burst into tears. "A man came into the *haus*. He tied me up and told her he'd kill all of us if she didn't go with him."

"Did you see his face?" Carter asked.

"*Nee.* He wore a mask."

Brett felt as if his heart had stopped. He'd known the killer had found her.

"Did you see anything? A car? Did you see how he got into the house?"

Katie spoke up. "I saw a maroon car parked across the road after Vera left to get something. I never thought it was strange. Our neighbors are *Englisch*."

"We'll have to talk with them." Brett turned to Carter. "If they saw the vehicle, maybe we can get a make or model. Or a license plate." Brett knelt beside Evie. "I'm going to go after your mom, okay? You stay here and wait."

"I will." She hugged him, then let Katie lead her away.

He and Carter marched to the house across the street. Music blared through the screen door. They had to knock three times before a man came to the door, wiping his hands on a kitchen dish towel.

His eyes popped wide-open when he saw the two police lieutenants standing on the porch. "Jason, turn that down."

The volume decreased. He opened the door and joined them. "Can I help you, Officers?"

"We've had a possible abduction in the area," Brett began. "Your neighbors said there was a strange car parked here, and we wondered if it was yours?"

"I've had my head under the kitchen sink all day. Wait." He shoved his head back into the house. "Jason! Come out here."

A boy of around twelve joined them. "Yeah?"

Brett repeated his question.

"Oh, yeah! I saw it. It was a beauty." He rattled off the make and model.

"Did you see the driver?"

"I did. He had a woman with him. An Amish woman." He wouldn't know Leila was in disguise.

"Was he wearing a mask?"

Jason gave him a strange look. "No."

Brett felt the first spark of hope. If the killer had removed his mask, maybe they could identify him.

Carter held up his phone. "My boss just sent us this picture. Is it this man?"

Jason peered at the phone for a few moments. "Yeah. That's him."

Without another word, Brett and Carter jogged back to the cruiser. Brett slid behind the wheel. Carter shot him a look, but Brett didn't care. He needed to find Leila before

Xavier Kelso did anything to her. Carter got into the passenger side without comment.

As Brett started the engine, Carter called the chief. “He’s taken Leila, boss. And the neighbor identified Xavier as the one who has her. They were in a maroon car.” He gave her the make and model.

Chief Kaiser was silent for a moment. “I have a stolen car that matches that description.”

Great. They had a license plate.

Brett’s phone buzzed. He glanced at it. Leila’s watch. “Hey! I got a text from Leila’s watch. She’s been carrying it in the pocket of the apron she was wearing this morning.”

“If it’s got a cell signal, we can trace it,” the chief said.

Brett hated sitting around doing nothing. But they had no idea which direction to go. Their radio burst into action as a BOLO for the maroon car went out. They sat for another five minutes before they had a signal from the watch.

“Head north for now,” the chief said. “We’re tracking the watch now.”

He shifted into Drive and pulled out. *Hold on, Leila. We’re coming to find you.*

He just prayed they would find her alive.

Leila glanced at the man beside her in the front seat of the car. The Brand Killer.

He looked familiar, but she didn’t recall ever meeting him. She studied him more closely. He looked similar to Shane, she realized. The gloves TBK always wore were on his hands, but he’d removed the mask when they’d left Vera’s house.

That didn’t strike her as a good thing. It told her he was confident she wouldn’t be alive to identify him.

His right hand held a gun shoved into her side.

"Who are you?" she whispered.

Anger flared across his face. "You don't remember me? Xavier Kelso."

The name sounded familiar, but she couldn't place it.

He thrust his face closer to hers. She flinched away. "My half brother, Shane, introduced us. I was even in a class with you."

She'd forgotten that Shane had a brother.

"Why did you kill my sister?" And why wasn't she tied up yet? Fear threatened to clog her throat.

"I thought it was you. I didn't realize you had a twin. I saw my brother kissing you one night. I asked you out, and you rejected me. But I knew you were meant for me. Yet you kissed him."

"I never kissed your brother." She gasped. She had never even gone out with Shane as friends back then.

He shrugged. "Like I said, I didn't know you had a twin."

The truth hit her. Shane had kissed Tara. She hadn't even realized they were dating.

"Shane was brokenhearted when his girlfriend died. That's when I knew he wasn't in love with you."

"Why did you kill the others?" She blurted. Did she really expect him to answer? But he surprised her.

"I couldn't get to you. But I had to punish you for rejecting me. And then I decided I liked killing those women. They all looked like you." He shook his head violently, his left hand tightening on the steering wheel. The gun pressed harder into her side. "But they weren't you. And I couldn't stop until you were punished."

There was no way she could reason with him. She saw that. The man was delusional. Did Shane have any idea that his brother was a murderer?

She doubted it. She'd seen no malice in his face.

After forty minutes of driving, Xavier pulled off on a quiet road with no houses. She didn't see any water. No lake or stream to dump a body, as was the Brand Killer's MO. Maybe he had other plans for her.

When he got out, she opened the door and started to run.

In seconds he caught her, yanking her by her hair, *kapp* and all. Pain seared through her head and she cried out.

"Oh, no, you don't. You're not getting away from me this time. I have it all planned out. Something extra special."

That's when she saw it. He had wood stacked up for a campfire. And next to it—

Her breath caught. Terror filled her. A brand with the number eight.

She broke away again. This time, when his feet pounded after her, he didn't grab her. She heard a slight whistle and then something hard crashed against the back of her head. She fell into darkness.

FIFTEEN

Her head ached.

Leila attempted to open her eyes, but her lids wouldn't obey her brain's commands. She tried lifting her head. Nope. Too painful. She groaned. Her left calf burned. Her head rested on something hard, like a metal box. Lifting her arms to feel around, she couldn't separate them.

Her wrists were bound together.

Panicking, she gasped in a harsh breath. A damp, stagnant odor hit the back of her tongue and she gagged. Where was she?

Once again, she tried to force her eyelids open. This time, she succeeded. When her eyes adjusted, she blinked. She was being held somewhere dark. Not a single of pinprick of light broke through the dank blackness surrounding her. Wherever she was, it wasn't stable. It dipped and swayed. Her stomach protested and she swallowed to keep the nausea at bay.

She kicked her legs out. As she suspected, she couldn't separate them. Xavier had secured them together, too. She tried kicking them in opposite directions, to stretch the duct tape that bound them. He'd used so many layers, her legs didn't budge even a centimeter apart.

They did kick some sort of barrier, though.

She stretched her trussed arms out. They hit a surface. When she followed the surface line, it curved over her head. She was in an area approximately four feet by three feet and only a couple of feet deep.

Her fingers trembled as they felt the hard metal ceiling. Suddenly, she knew exactly where she was. She wasn't in a box. She was in a trunk. Xavier was driving her somewhere.

As if to prove her theory, the vehicle hit some kind of large bump, possibly a pothole. Her head slammed against the metal box it was resting on. Something shifted inside it. Probably a tool or tackle box.

Maybe she could feel around for the cord that would release the trunk. Her fingers were awkward, both from the fear making them shake and from being taped together. Moving them the way she needed without the other hand getting in the way proved difficult. She winced when something sliced into her pointer finger. The dark prevented her from seeing what she'd cut it on. Within seconds, she felt blood dripping down it.

She couldn't worry about that. If Xavier had his way, she'd be dead soon. What would happen to Evie?

She rested her pounding head on its hard pillow for a moment and prayed for Evie's safety. "God, if it's Your will, I beg to be rescued. Please, Lord."

She wanted to ask Him to send Brett but didn't want to be greedy. However God planned to save her, she'd accept.

And if He didn't?

She had to accept that, as well.

But that didn't mean she needed to give up and let this creep kill her without a fight. She pressed her lips together and began searching for the release cord again. Her fingers slipped over a round hole.

Yes! She brushed the edges of the hole and felt only the frayed end of a stubble of twine.

Xavier had severed the release cord.

Despair flooded her soul. He'd outmaneuvered her. Until he opened the trunk, she would remain stuck inside. But if he opened it, maybe she could fight him. She tried to twist so she could get an angle to kick him.

It was no use.

She couldn't maneuver herself around in the tiny space with her hands and legs tied. What was left?

The box beneath her head! If it was a toolbox, maybe she could find a screwdriver or a hammer, something to defend herself with. Scooting deeper into the truck, she fumbled with the box. She managed to move it in front of her, which helped her flip the two latches holding the lid shut.

Inside the box, she felt the various items, half expecting to impale her fingers on a fishhook. Instead, she nearly wept with joy when her hands encountered various metal-handled instruments. She wasn't a tool aficionado, but she recognized the shapes of several wrenches, pliers, screwdrivers and a hammer. The screwdrivers were smaller than she'd like. The hammer, though, was hefty. It might do some damage.

The vehicle slowed to a stop, although the engine remained on. This might be it. Her only chance of escape. She tensed inside the trunk, ready to battle for her life when Xavier opened the trunk.

Except he didn't.

She could hear him messing around in the front of the car. Then it started moving again. From the angle, it seemed to be going downhill, then it hit a cushioned bump. What in the world?

"Enjoy your swim, Leila." Xavier's voice reached her from outside the trunk.

What did he mean by that?

In a moment, the trunk cooled as freezing water pooled around her legs. The engine stalled.

Leila's heart pounded in her ears. She wouldn't get a chance to fight Xavier off. He'd trussed her up like a cow going to the slaughter and had driven the car into the water. She was going to drown, with no one aware of where she was.

Fear clawed at her throat. The water seemed to be getting deeper. It was a slow process, but eventually, she knew the vehicle would be completely submerged.

Hadn't she seen that people could escape a trunk by going through the inside of the car? It was her only hope now. She worked to roll to her other side. She felt along the back wall. One side seemed to be more flexible than the other. If she could hammer her way through, maybe she could get into the main part of the car and open the doors. Or crawl through a window.

With the hammer, she pounded on the panel. Every two or three hits, she felt around. It was dented, but still in place. She braced herself and slammed the hammer against it again as hard as the small space and her bound limbs would allow.

The wall gave a little. Leila sobbed. *Please, oh, please, God.* She hit it again.

A sliver of light cut through the darkness. She doubled her efforts, despite her aching muscles and the cold water rushing under her, soaking her legs and left side. Pain echoed in her head with every strike, but she continued pounding until the panel fell in.

Leila wiggled through the gap made by the broken panel. The water was deeper inside the car, but at least it wasn't dark. She sat on the back seat, the water to her knees, and glanced around. She was in a lake of some kind. Not one she recognized. A lump lodged in her throat. Somehow, she was going to have to get out of the car and into the water.

How, she didn't know. But she had no choice. If she wanted to see her baby again, if she wanted to see Brett again, she had to do it. Even though water terrified her. There were no other options. A Scripture verse came to mind. She couldn't think of the book or the exact words, but the verse said something about God not giving us a spirit of fear.

It was time to be bold and face her deepest fears.

There were no boats or swimmers around. Wherever she was, it was isolated. She saw a boat ramp and realized Xavier had driven the car down it into the water.

She grabbed the door handle with both hands and pulled. Nothing. It was locked. And the windows were electric, so she couldn't roll them down.

She was so cold.

Don't give up. Think.

An idea came to her, but first, she needed to be able to move. The tilt of the car made sitting on the bench seat awkward. She braced her feet on the floorboard, shivering. The water covering her lower legs blurred her view of the tape and soaked through the hem of the dress, weighing it down. She bent closer and shuddered. Bile rose in her throat. She swallowed, hard.

On her left calf, the number eight peeked up at her.

She'd been branded. Just like Tara and the other six women who had taken her place since Xavier began his grisly hunt.

I can deal with this later. First, I need to free myself.

She clenched her teeth and got to work. Using the claw side of the hammer, she ripped through the duct tape binding her ankles. Xavier had wound it around several times. Finally, her feet were free. They prickled like a million needles were piercing her skin as the blood flowed back into the tender feet.

She tried to hold the hammer between her knees to do the same to the duct tape on her wrists, but the hammer slipped out and fell under the driver's seat. As she bent to grab it, her face met the water.

Leila pulled her head away from the water, gasping. She swallowed a mouthful and coughed. Her fear of drowning took hold and she couldn't move. She couldn't get the hammer.

She hadn't swum since before Tara died. What if she made it out of the car and she couldn't remember how?

She needed to keep going. She couldn't stop. Now that her feet could move, she climbed to the middle console.

No way. The water was deeper in the front seat.

Trying the window panel wouldn't work. It was gone. Xavier had ripped it out of the car. He'd taken no chances.

That's when she noticed the panel at the top of the car. This vehicle had a sunroof. If she could manage to crawl out of the sunroof, maybe she could get to freedom. She wrenched the cover back.

Then she gasped. She had to blink to make sure she wasn't imagining what she saw.

Xavier, the arrogant fool, had left the sunroof *open*. No doubt he intended to flood the car even faster.

She grabbed the edges and pulled herself up through the hole. Then she sat for a moment on the edge, considering her options. There was only one: She'd have to swim for shore. She wasn't that far out, but the car had been carried in too far for her to merely walk out.

"No!" The sound of Xavier's scream echoed in her ears.

Leila whirled, nearly unseating herself, to find Xavier standing on the dock next to the boat ramp, his face screwed into a mask of rage. Had she been faced with those eyes the first time they had met, she'd have run in the opposite direction as fast as she could.

"I want to watch you die!" he yelled.

He grabbed a gun that had been shoved in his waistband and aimed it at her. She had a split second to react before he shot. She dived into the water, praying she'd be able to swim away from him. The other side was farther than she'd ever swum before.

Her life was completely in God's hands.

"Brett, do you even know where we're going?" Carter asked, his left hand braced on the console and his right against the door as Brett took a corner.

"I'm not sure. I'm just following what they tell me."

Chief Kaiser's voice sounded through the radio. "Gentlemen, the signal has stopped in the lake."

The chief had been tracking the signal from Leila's smart watch. She had first led them to a field, where they found a small campfire, a large wrench with some blood on it and a brand.

Rage had pulsed through him. There was no doubt that her abductor planned to kill her. Victim number eight. They had to find her before that could happen.

For a scary mile or two, the signal had been lost. The car must have gone through a dead zone. But then it was picked up again. He'd been following the chief's directions ever since, tapping his fingers against the wheel, wondering how much time she had left. Sending up a constant silent prayer for her. Not since his father killed his mom had he felt this helpless.

"At the lake?" Brett asked, his throat tight. *No, no, no.* She couldn't die. Not her. He'd gladly give his own life to save her.

He slammed his foot on the gas. The engine roared in response. Carter yelped when the cruiser leaped forward. Brett ignored it all. He needed to get to Leila.

Lord, protect her. I love her. I don't know how it happened, but it did. Please, Lord, let me get to her in time.

He pushed the vehicle as fast as he could safely drive it. Beside him, Carter sat silently, his hand gripping the handle near the top of the door like a lifeline.

"Sorry, buddy," Brett said.

"Just drive. I can handle it."

Every second dragged by. What was happening now? The excruciating agony of not knowing if Leila was dead or alive felt like a knife to his heart. She feared water. With good reason. He had no doubt that Xavier planned on killing her at the lake. TBK was known for drowning his victims. Brett pounded his fist on the steering wheel. He had to block the images of her pain and suffering out of his mind. If he focused on the possible scenarios, he'd falter. She needed him to be logical and find her. He followed the chief's instructions, turning off onto a paved road that led to the local beaches and to the boat dock.

When he reached the entrance gate, he groaned.

A man in a brown uniform sat in the small gatekeeper booth, chomping on a wad of bubblegum. "Morning."

Brett flashed his badge. "Sir. I need you to open this gate. We have an emergency by the dock."

"There's only one car here."

"I know."

Confused, the man obliged and opened the gate. The arm lifted slowly. The moment it was high enough for the cruiser to pass, Brett pressed the gas pedal and rushed by. He had to slow to take the one-lane road.

Finally, the lake came into view. His blood ran cold. Beside him, Carter exclaimed. It was a scene out of a horror movie. Several hundred feet out into the blue water, a car swayed, partially submerged.

There was a popping sound.

"There!" Carter pointed.

Xavier stood on the dock shooting into the water. A second later, a familiar head burst out of the water. Leila! She bobbed there for a short time, then went under again. But she was alive. Xavier raised the gun to take another shot at her. Brett floored the vehicle, screeching to a halt at the front of the boat ramp. With the motor running he jumped from it, snatching his own gun from his holster at the same time. Carter jumped from the other side, his hand at the radio on his shoulder.

Brett let his friend call for backup. He couldn't take his eyes off Xavier.

"Xavier Kelso, put down your gun!" He snapped the safety off and aimed it directly at Xavier, never stopping his forward advance.

"No! She has to die!" Xavier pivoted to take another shot at Leila.

Brett flexed his fingers on the trigger. He barely felt the recoil when the bullet left the chamber. He aimed for Xavier's hand, but Xavier shifted at the last moment. The bullet hit him in the chest and he went down. He knew immediately the man was dead. He was sorry about that. He'd tried to take him alive.

Brett handed his Glock to Carter and took a running leap off the dock into the water. Leila had vanished. He sucked in a deep breath and dived underwater, his arms outstretched, feeling for her. He swam around and around, only coming up when his lungs were ready to burst, before diving deep again. Finally, his open palm connected with an arm.

Leila! Her hands were still tied together by the duct tape, but her legs were limp. She wasn't kicking. Frantically, he lifted her head above water. But she didn't take in any of the air. He swam with her to the shore and heaved her body onto the cement boat ramp.

"She's not breathing!" he screamed.

Carter dropped down on her other side. He had a pocket knife in his hand, which he used to slice through the tape. The motionless woman's hands fell to her sides.

Brett began CPR, keeping his gaze trained on Leila's pale face and blue lips as he did compressions.

"Come on, Leila. Come on. Don't you die on me now. Please, open your eyes." His back and shoulders burned. He didn't care. All that mattered was the woman lying so still on the ground in front of him.

After what felt like an eternity, her eyes popped open and she began to gag. He rolled her over onto her side and Leila vomited a torrent of water.

Gently, Brett raised Leila, supporting her back against his chest and using his body to block her view of Xavier's body. As horrible as it felt knowing he'd taken a life, deep down, there was a sense of relief that the Brand Killer couldn't ever kill another innocent woman.

Brett peered down at Leila. "Did he shoot you?"

She coughed. "No. He tried. I got so tired of treading

water. And when I went under to get away from him, I kept swallowing water."

It chilled him, how close she'd come to drowning.

"Are you hurt anywhere?" He scanned her. When his eyes caught sight of the brand on her leg, the fury reignited inside him.

"Carter!" Brett called and pointed to the brand. Carter's eyes followed the trajectory of his finger and widened when he saw it.

Leila reached up and took his hand, bringing it back down to her side. "It's okay. Yes, he branded me, but I survived. Thanks to you. God used you to answer my prayers." She reached up and touched her head. "He hit me on the back of the head with something. But I'll heal."

Brett remembered the wrench they had found at the campfire. He gently touched the back of her head. When his fingers found the large knot, she winced.

"It hurts, but I'll be fine, Brett," she murmured, a smile ghosting across her lips before her eyes closed.

Ignoring protocol, and with his best friend watching the whole scene, Brett bent over and lightly kissed the top of her head.

"The ambulance is on the way," Carter announced, looking at his phone.

In his arms, Leila whispered, "I need to see my daughter."

"I made sure she was taken care of before we came," Brett assured her. "After you get looked at, we'll get her to the hospital so she can see you."

"Do me a favor," she breathed.

"Anything you need," Brett responded, meaning it with his whole heart.

"Call my dad. I think it's time we hashed things out."

"I will. At the first possible moment I'll call him."

He heard the sirens. Within two minutes, the ambulance arrived on scene. The paramedics took her from his arms, leaving him bereft.

He shook himself and turned to Carter. "As soon as the coroner takes the body, let's get back to the station."

Carter raised his eyebrows. "Wow. I thought I'd have to drag you there."

"I want to get everything done. Once I know that this case is wrapped up and I have finished my part in it, I want to go be with Leila at the hospital. If I went there now, I'd just make a nuisance of myself in the waiting room."

"Yeah. You'd pace. You always pace like a caged animal when you're anxious."

He couldn't deny it. But only Carter knew him well enough to say it.

The coroner showed up a few minutes later. It didn't take long. The bullet wound in the man's chest was clearly the cause of death. He didn't have the same approachable air Deanna had, but the coroner worked efficiently. That was all Brett cared about. Once he took charge of Xavier's body, Brett called the chief to update her on the status.

"I've released the other suspect, with our apologies," the chief told him when he was finished.

"Carter and I are heading in."

He hung up and walked to the cruiser, suddenly exhausted. "Carter, you want to drive? I'm all in."

"Sure."

Brett slid into the passenger seat. He wanted to close his eyes and sleep, but he was still on duty. Besides, he knew if he did, he'd relive the horror of finding Leila's lifeless body in the lake again.

He'd never forget that moment.

Nor would he ever stop being grateful that she was alive and well.

Leila zipped another bag and set it on the growing pile. She reached for another bag but let her hand drop when someone knocked on her door.

Walking to the front door, she looked through the peephole. Brett. He'd stopped by the hospital to see her the night before, but she was still groggy from the medication they'd given her to alleviate the pain in her head. She was grateful that was the only injury she'd suffered. She'd been given a prescription for antibiotics and strict instructions on how to care for the wound so it wouldn't become infected. After the nurse had gone over them and handed her a stack of papers to sign, Brett had driven her home and Michaela had come over to sleep in her guest room until morning. She'd gone to work several hours ago.

She needed to talk with him, but this would be a hard conversation. Best to get it over with. She swung open the door and unlocked the screen. "Come on in."

When he entered, she fidgeted. "Can I get you something to drink?"

"Nah. I just got done talking with the chief. She said you'd taken a leave of absence, effective immediately."

Leila tensed. "Yes. I did."

"I don't mean to pry. But I got worried."

He didn't continue. But she heard the question in his voice. If anyone deserved to know her feelings, it was Brett Talbot.

"I'm sorry you were worried. But after everything that happened the last few days, I realized I'm in no frame of mind to go back to photographing crime scenes. Something about being the actual victim has messed with my objectivity."

He nodded, the corners of his mouth pulling down into a thoughtful frown. "Yeah, I can see that. Anything I can do to help?"

Actually, he was part of the problem. Of course, she couldn't say it that way. But she did need to address it.

"Here's the thing, Brett. My emotions are really mixed up right now. I feel like you and I have gotten really close, and I have feelings for you." He opened his mouth, but she held up one finger to halt whatever he planned on saying. "I don't want to talk about those feelings right now because I'm not sure if it's just what happened or if those feelings are true."

She'd never forget the hurt look in his eyes before they became shuttered again. Blank. For a moment, she didn't think he was going to say anything. Finally, he sighed and ran a hand through his military-short hair. "I guess I can understand that. I have feelings for you, too. However, I'm fairly certain that my feelings are real. I've been through enough hard cases in my career and I have never fallen for any of my colleagues or the victims. But I can give you some space if you need it."

His gaze settled on the bags she had in the middle of her living room. "I take it you're planning on going somewhere?"

"Yeah. I talked with my dad. Thanks for calling him, by the way. He's invited Evie and me to spend some time with him and Kelly, his new wife. I've decided it was time that I got to know her. And it's time to mend fences with him."

"When will you be back?"

Her throat throbbed with the tears she wouldn't shed. "I don't know. It might be a week. Maybe longer. In all actuality, I'm not sure if I can come back to this house, if I can come back to this life. I think I will. But I need to figure out the next step."

"I just need to know, if you realize that your feelings for me are real, can I still be part of your life, no matter where you end up?"

"What if I decide my feelings are real but I don't want to come back to Pennsylvania? What if I need to stay in Colorado?"

He shrugged. "Well, I suppose I could find a new job."

That shocked her. She searched his face. He was serious. "But your life is here."

"I have no family. Carter is my best friend, but we'll always be close. You and Evie mean the world to me."

She bit her lip. This was so much harder than she'd expected it would be. "I can't promise anything. But I will let you know the moment I make any decisions."

He moved closer. His arms gently encircled her waist and tugged her to him. "I will wait as long as you need. Just know this, Leila Britton. I will not betray you or forget you. You will always be my first priority. Come back to me when you can. We'll figure the rest out later."

He leaned in, giving her time to back away. Then he kissed her, slowly, showing her wordlessly that he meant what he said.

When he backed away, she touched her lips, still tingling from his kiss, and watched him walk out the door, knowing that the next move was hers.

SIXTEEN

Leila went into the kitchen and found her dad and Kelly chatting over coffee and bagels. She braced herself for the difficult conversation she knew had to happen.

"Hey!" Her dad rose to his feet and pulled her into a gentle hug. "There are more bagels, including the blueberry ones you like. I didn't want to wake you. You were up late last night."

She hugged him back before moving over to grab her breakfast. While it was in the toaster, she poured a cup of coffee, added cream and sugar, and then joined them at the table once her bagel was ready.

"I see Evie already ate." She pointed at the empty cereal bowl.

Kelly chuckled. "Oh, yes. She was down bright and early. She's watching a unicorn movie right now."

"That's good. I wanted to talk with both of you."

Her dad tensed in his chair. "Is everything okay?"

She waved a hand in the air. "Fine. Fine. I wanted to thank you for your hospitality. Confronting Tara's killer, and learning that I was his actual target, hit me hard. I also want to apologize for not giving you a fair chance before. I shut you out, Dad. And, Kelly, I never let you get close. I regret that."

Kelly set a warm hand on hers. "Oh, honey. Never mind that. We know it's been a hard few years for you. We're so grateful that you've let us in now."

Overcome with emotions, Leila cleared her throat. She'd lost so much time. "I will always regret not doing it sooner."

"None of that," her dad said. "We've all made mistakes. But we can't hold on to them."

"Yes. And that brings me to the next topic. It's time for me to return home."

Silence blanketed the room. In the background, she heard Evie's movie playing.

"So soon?" Kelly murmured.

"I'm afraid so. I've been gone nearly two weeks. But I have a job to get back to. I realized that I couldn't just walk away, not yet. And I haven't visited Tara's grave in a long time. I need to do that. And then…" She couldn't bring herself to say it. To openly wish for something that may never happen.

"You want to go back to Brett, your sturdy police officer."

"Dad." Now her face was on fire. "He's not mine."

"You love him, though. Don't you?"

Had she been so obvious?

"I do. And I think—I'm almost certain—he loves me, too. But even if he doesn't, I need to get back to my life."

Her dad put his hand over hers. "Whatever you need. I visited Tara's grave while I was in Sterling Ridge. But I'll come with you if you want."

"No. Thanks. I have to do this alone."

"Well, honey, you know we're always here for you. And if you ever want to visit, the door's open. Doesn't matter when or for how long."

"Thanks, Dad. Kelly. And I want you to know the same goes for coming to see us. We'd love to have you."

It was amazing how quickly events happened once the decision had been made. Within twenty-four hours, Leila had booked a flight for herself and Evie. Kelly helped them pack. Her dad drove them to the airport. After a final round of hugs, they boarded the airplane and returned home. Evie stared out the window the entire flight, mesmerized.

When Leila opened her front door, it was dinner time. She made Evie some macaroni and cheese. While her daughter ate, she called Michaela.

"Leila! What's up?"

"Hi, Michaela. Evie and I just got back this evening." They chatted for a few minutes. After they'd caught up, Leila cleared her throat. "I was wondering. Would you be able to watch Evie for about an hour or so after work tomorrow?"

"Absolutely!"

Leila let out a breath. "Thanks. Before I left, Katie had told me she was planning on staying with Vera for the rest of July."

She wouldn't be back for another four days.

The next afternoon, Leila let Michaela inside. Evie ran in and hugged the pretty officer.

"I appreciate this, Michaela. I need to go to the cemetery and run some errands."

Michaela nodded, her smile sincere. "No problem. Take your time."

Leila kissed her daughter and reminded her to be good, then headed to her car.

Sooner than she was ready, the cemetery entrance loomed in front of her. It had been years, but she had no trouble finding Tara's grave. She brushed the dirt off the flat headstone.

"Hey, sis. Sorry it's been so long. I guess I haven't been a very good sister."

She spent thirty minutes at her sister's grave, pouring out all the feelings she'd kept inside for so long. On the headstone, her parents had had a Bible verse carved. John 11:25–26. "Jesus said unto her, I am the resurrection and the life: he that believeth in me, though he were dead, yet shall he live."

Warmth settled in her chest. It felt like God was directly comforting her, letting her know Tara was safe in His arms. Carefully setting the flowers she'd brought on the grave, she left to return home. Silent tears dripped down her face, but her soul was at peace.

She waited until Monday morning, though, before putting in a call to her boss. He was overjoyed that she'd decided to return and promised to put her back in the rotation immediately.

Now all she had to do was inform Brett. Tension twisted her gut. She wasn't quite ready to do that. Not because she didn't want to see him. She did. She craved to hear his voice again and see his beloved face.

No, she needed to brace herself for the possibility that he might have changed his mind.

Tomorrow, she decided. *I'll contact him tomorrow.*

Tonight, I'll pray.

Brett stared at his computer screen, not seeing the report he had opened up and was supposed to send to his chief before his shift ended.

Two weeks. It had been two weeks since Brett had last seen Leila. It had been the longest two weeks of his life. He hadn't called or texted. Nothing. But then, neither had she. She'd asked for time, and he'd given it to her, but now he wondered if he was a fool for giving in so easily. How long could he go on like this? He was barely living. He'd poured himself into his work—so much so that even Carter had commented on his heightened intensity. Brett hadn't told him what was going on in his heart, but he was sure Carter understood. The only time Brett slowed down was when he finally exhausted himself and collapsed into bed late at night.

Even then, peace didn't come. It was as if he was missing a part of himself. Physically, he was in superb shape, but his heart ached to see her again. Or to even hear her voice. And then there was Evie. Man, he missed that sweet little girl. She'd crawled into his heart and made a home there without him even realizing it. He'd had no chance against either of them.

Carter sauntered over and lazily dropped himself into his chair. He took a loud sip of coffee, smacked his lips and raised his eyebrows at Brett. "Well?"

"Well, what?" Brett asked, internally wincing at how defensive his tone was.

"So, you haven't heard the news?" Carter drawled—and then he waited.

"I haven't heard anything. What's going on?" Brett prompted, mildly curious. If he waited long enough, he knew Carter would tell him.

"I just heard that our lovely forensic photographer is back on duty. She'll be joining us at crime scenes again. Starting tomorrow." Carter smiled, but his laser-sharp gaze scrutinized Brett's every expression.

Brett had started to reach for his own coffee mug, but at his friend's revelation, his hand froze in midair.

"She's back? How is she?" Questions blazed in his mind. "And Evie? Are they okay? Did—"

Carter shook his head and held up his hands. "Buddy, I don't know how she is. But I'm assuming things are okay, because she's back."

Brett's mind was a garbled mess. He'd feared she'd never return. These last days, he'd expected to hear she'd resigned. But now she was back. *I should go see her.*

"You should," Carter agreed.

He hadn't realized he'd said those words out loud, but he didn't care that Carter had heard them. Now, though, he doubted himself.

"No—no, I shouldn't. I told her I'd give her time. Going to see her isn't giving her time."

"Correction. You've given her time. And now she's returned. She's coming back to work. She's going to see you anyway. Why wait until you meet at a crime scene? Go see her. Check on her. Make sure everything's okay."

"I just don't want to cause her any more anguish than she's already suffered." *Or face rejection a second time.* Because even though she'd admitted to having feelings for him when she left, it had felt exactly like a rejection, no matter how he'd tried to convince himself otherwise.

"Look," Carter said, "I've seen the way you two look at each other. If I had to guess, I'd say she's been missing you as much as you've been pretending not to miss her."

Brett snorted. Yeah, Carter had a point. Especially about pretending. He couldn't even deny what his friend was saying. He'd worked himself into exhaustion just so he wouldn't have to think about her. But even then, she was always there—and when he slept, she found him in his dreams.

He wasn't fooling anyone.

"All right. You have a point. I'll go see her. And if she

indicates she doesn't want to see me, I'll back off." If he could. He drank some coffee to hide his growing agitation.

"That's a good plan. But I really don't think you have anything to worry about. That woman feels as strongly about you as you do about her. I have no doubt." Carter smirked. "Just remember—I want to be best man at your wedding."

Brett choked as a mouthful of coffee went down the wrong way.

"Sorry."

Funny, he didn't sound sorry.

"I'm good. You're moving a little faster than I had in mind." Brett shook his head. "First, I want to make sure she'll talk to me. Then maybe I'll ask her on a date. After that, we'll see how it goes."

Carter's smile was smug, but Brett didn't mind. And his friend wasn't wrong. If Leila would see him, he fully planned to court her until she agreed to be his wife and stay with him until death do them part.

But it wouldn't do to get ahead of himself. Too many ifs stood between him and the ending he wanted. He'd never know, though, if he didn't try.

The last two hours of his shift were interminable. Now that he knew she was back—and that he had made plans to see her—the hope buzzing around inside him made it hard to sit still and finish his reports. But not doing his duty wasn't in Brett's character. He buckled down and completed the work the chief had asked for.

When his shift ended, he ignored the amazed glances from coworkers as he cleared off the top of his desk and headed for the door. It was very rare for him to leave on time—especially over the last couple of weeks—but today he was on a mission.

"You leaving?" Joe asked.

"Sure am. Got things to do, places to be."

Carter nodded. "See you tomorrow."

He sketched a wave at Carter and strode out of the building. He barely noticed the chill in the air. Despite it being the middle of summer, they were getting a slight break from the heat wave. The scent in the air told him it was going to rain.

It reminded him of the day he'd met Leila.

He drove the familiar route and parked behind her vehicle. He didn't waste time second-guessing himself once a decision was made. He turned off the engine and hopped out. After locking his cruiser, Brett marched up to the door and raised his hand to hit the bell, but she was already there, waiting for him.

He was here.

Leila had wondered if she should text him, or call him, to let him know she was back, but both had seemed so impersonal. She was never her best on the phone. She preferred to connect in person. Especially when it mattered.

Her stomach quivered like Jell-O as she watched Brett's confident stride to her door. Only the tightness of his jaw informed her that he wasn't feeling as sure of himself as he projected.

That made two of them.

When his eyes met hers, joy exploded inside her. She struggled to tamp it down. Just because he was here didn't mean that they would be able to pick up where they left off. He might have decided she was more trouble than she was worth, or that the feelings they'd had were the result of being in forced proximity and facing danger together.

She hoped not. Could she stay and work with him if all he wanted was to be colleagues?

She was strong, but she didn't know if she was that strong.

"Are you going to let me in?"

She heard the amusement in his voice and flushed. "Oh, sorry. Here, come in."

She unlocked the screen and opened it before stepping out of the way. She never left any doors or windows unlocked anymore. She hated that fear controlled her even that much, but she wouldn't risk her daughter's life.

"Brett!" Evie darted into the room and wrapped her arms around his legs. He laughed and squatted down to look her in the eyes.

"Hey. How's my favorite munchkin?"

Evie giggled. "I'm okay. I got to stay with my grandpa for a few days."

"That's good." His tone remained casual, but his gaze searched Leila's face. She read the question he didn't want to ask.

"It's been good getting reacquainted." She'd tell him more once Evie was out of earshot. "Evie, why don't you go and play in your room for a few minutes until dinner?"

"Okay." Evie didn't quite pout, but it was a close call. "Is Brett staying for dinner?"

She bit her lip and looked at him, still unsure what he wanted. "Will you?"

His grin lit up the room. "I'd love to."

"Yay!" Evie hugged him again, then dashed to her room to play.

An awkward silence settled between Leila and Brett, heavy with all the things that needed to be said. The longing to rush over and embrace him as freely as her daughter had nearly overwhelmed Leila.

Instead, she pivoted toward the kitchen and waved for him to follow her. She hadn't planned a fancy meal for dinner. Spaghetti squash with meatballs, biscuits and a salad. Fortunately, she'd made enough for Brett to join them. She'd have to fix something else for her lunch instead of leftovers, but she didn't mind. The pleasure of having him in her space again was enough.

"I heard you're coming back to work." He took the plates from her hands and set them on the table.

She twisted a lock of hair around her fingers. "I am. I decided I've taken enough time off and I need to go on with my life."

"Does that life include me?"

Leaning back against the countertop, she faced him. "I hope so. I want it to. But I didn't want to make any assumptions."

He crossed the three feet between them and took hold of her hands. "These past two weeks have been torture. I tried to give you space, like you asked. But it was hard. I drove past your house a few times, just to see if you were home."

"I went to my dad's." Why had she said that? He already knew it.

"So I heard."

She sighed. "How do I explain this? After Xavier tried to kill me, I was filled with so much rage and so confused. I think the fact that Xavier was dead angered me. I felt like there was no closure. I knew I wasn't capable of making any rational decisions. At first, I just planned to take time off. But when my dad invited me, I really felt like God wanted me to go. And I'm glad I did. We're not one hundred percent, but I think we've begun to heal our relationship."

His hand brushed a curl away from her cheek, leaving a tingling trail in its wake. “I’m glad to hear that. I know it must have been hard not having a father around. Especially after your husband died.”

“Yeah, but looking back, I don’t think he’d have approved of Will. They would have butted heads on several issues.” She shook her head. That wasn’t something they needed to get into now. “Anyway, I got my act together and realized that I needed to be here. I missed my life. My work.”

“Is that all?”

She shook her head and tightened her hands in his. “No. Most of all, I missed you. I’m not over everything that happened. I have nightmares. But I refuse to let fear—to let *him*—control how I live my life.”

Brett leaned in and rested his forehead against hers. Leila inhaled deeply, relishing his fresh scent. It grounded her. “I missed you and Evie, too. After living without you, I know my own heart. Leila, I love you.”

Tears blurred her vision. She blinked them away. “I love you, too.”

He stepped closer into her space. “I hoped you felt the same. I couldn’t imagine losing you, not now.”

Leila gently pulled her right hand free and brought it to his cheek. “You won’t lose me. All I want is here. I am so thankful God brought me back to you.”

Brett backed away. “I have something for you.”

“What?”

He pulled out a yellow envelope. “Since the case was closed, I asked the chief if I could remove this from the evidence room.”

He took her hand and dumped the contents into her palm. She gasped. In the center of her hand lay Tara’s necklace.

"Brett." Tears misted her eyes. She couldn't say anything more. Her heart was too full.

In response, Brett closed the remaining gap between them and caught her lips in a gentle kiss. In it, she felt all the love and acceptance she'd waited for her entire life. Finally, she'd truly come home.

EPILOGUE

Seven months later

Balloons were everywhere, in a variety of shades of pink and purple. A crowd of children giggled and bounced in their seats, waiting for their piece of cake. Evie sat in the midst of all the happy chaos, a sparkly tiara on her brown curls, a huge smile on her sweet face. Leila blinked away tears. Her baby was five now.

"Happy birthday, Evie!" She set the cake in front of her daughter, the five candles already lit. The flames danced. "Make a wish and blow out the candles."

Evie's face scrunched in concentration, then she nodded, apparently satisfied with her wish. When her gaze cut over to Brett, Leila flushed, pretty sure she'd just wished for him to be her daddy. Her daughter had been making such comments to Leila for the past two months.

Fortunately, she had kept those comments strictly between the two of them.

Brett winked at Evie.

Leila's stomach plummeted in embarrassment. Maybe she hadn't been as discreet as her mother hoped. Her hand reached up and played with her necklace. After Brett had returned Tara's to her, she'd taken both the necklaces in and had them specially welded together. It was like having a piece of her sister with her always.

Brett grinned at Leila, his gaze so full of masculine appreciation that her embarrassment vanished. She hoped he'd ask her soon. She knew he loved her. They had talked about the future in the past few months. Both of them were ready to move on and create a family of their own. They knew that life had risks, but love was worth it.

Evie blew out the candles and everyone clapped.

"Leila, can I help with the cake and ice cream?" Kelly stood at her side.

"Sure. I'd like the help." She'd discovered Kelly had a warm, generous heart once she'd finally stopped shutting out her father and his new wife. In fact, they were becoming friends. How much she'd missed having family in the past few years.

"She's like a princess among her subjects," her dad commented, grinning at his granddaughter.

Leila nodded as Brett joined them. Her boyfriend—it still tickled her to refer to a grown man as her boyfriend when he was so much more—slung an arm around her waist. She allowed herself to lean into him as she continued her conversation.

"I'm glad you and Kelly convinced me to send her to preschool. She's made friends and is having the time of her life. But I'll be the first to admit, it was hard sending her away after all that had happened."

Brett leaned down and kissed her forehead. "At least your nightmares are finally fading."

"How often do you have them now?" her dad asked.

She shrugged. "Every few weeks. Mostly after a stressful day or when I go to a brutal crime scene."

"I hate that you have to deal with that." Her dad frowned. "Now that *he's* gone, can't you find a different line of work?"

Her dad refused to refer to Tara's killer by name. He wouldn't give him the notoriety he'd craved.

"I could, but I don't want to. I like my job. It brings me satisfaction to know I'm helping bring justice to victims and their families. I know it sounds silly."

"Not silly at all." Brett, as always, was her champion. More than anyone else, he understood her desire to be a force for good.

Her father laid a gentle hand on her shoulder. "You know that I will stand with you—whatever you decide to do. But I'm your father, and I'll always want to protect you, to keep you safe."

His voice softened. "I kind of suspect that's not going to be my role for much longer."

He cast a sly glance at Brett, a knowing twinkle in his eyes. Then, with a warm smile, he patted her shoulder once more and reached for Kelly's hand. The two of them wandered off into the crowd, hand in hand, their laughter melting in with the other conversations.

Leila smiled, her chest tightening with emotion. A soft laugh escaped her lips.

"Hey," Brett said, brushing her arm gently. "The party looks like a success."

"Yeah." She nodded, glancing around at the gathering of family and friends. "I didn't realize how much I missed my dad until these last few months. I appreciate that he's not really pressuring me to leave my job. Before this, he would have."

"Try to see it from his side, though," Brett said softly, sliding an arm around her waist. "Even though you're thirty-one years old, you're still his little girl."

Leila leaned into him, resting her head on his shoulder. She closed her eyes for a moment, drawing strength from his steady presence.

"I know," she whispered. "I think…seeing Evie grow up so fast—it makes me more aware of how he must feel. I'm just glad to have him back in my life."

Brett slipped his arm from her waist to take her hand in his. Together, they went back to the party.

Once Evie and the kids had finished the cake, it was time for the presents. Evie opened each of the gifts and her family and friends oohed and ahhed over each one. Until there was only one very small gift left.

Evie grinned and waved Leila and Brett over.

"Let me take the camera."

Confused, Leila handed the camera to Kelly. "Sure."

Brett joined her at Evie's side.

"What's wrong, Evie?"

"Nothing, Mommy. But this one isn't for me."

She handed the tiny box to Brett, who was looking a little nervous. Leila's stomach flipped over. The crowd around them murmured and stilled.

Brett nearly dropped the box Evie shoved at him. He couldn't recall the last time he'd felt this nervous. One glance at Leila's face eased those feelings. The confusion had melted into hesitant anticipation. Her cheeks flushed, making her brown eyes sparkle, and for a moment, he lost himself in her gaze. Then a tiny hand nudged his arm.

Brett grinned at Evie before dropping down to one knee. The women present gasped. When he pulled out a second box with Evie written in big letters on top of it, the little girl clapped in delight.

"Leila, Evie, you are the most important people in my

life. You make me want to make the world a better place to keep you safe. You make me want to be a better man. I love you both. Leila, would you be my wife, so I can love and protect you always?"

Leila nodded. "Oh, yes. I will marry you. I love you, too." He gently put the ring on her finger, then kissed her hand.

"She wondered if you'd ever ask," Evie whispered loudly.

Everyone laughed.

Then he turned to Evie and held out the second box, which had a charm bracelet with a single heart-shaped charm on it. "What do you say, Evie? Will you be my little girl forever?"

Her big eyes widened. "If you and Mommy get married, you'd be my daddy."

"I would. Are you okay with that?"

"Yes!" she shouted, throwing her arms around his neck. He heard some sniffles in the crowd.

Still holding Evie, he stood and brought Leila into his embrace to a solid round of applause.

"Mommy!"

Leila's eyes were bright with tears. She smiled at her daughter. "Yes, sweetie?"

"My wish came true!"

A few minutes later, the children went into the other room to watch a movie. The adults swarmed around Brett and Leila to congratulate them. Brett couldn't stop grinning. She'd said yes. He was engaged to the woman of his dreams and would soon have a family of his own.

The future would come with challenges, but he knew he wouldn't face them alone.

The next hour flew by. Parents arrived to pick up their children, friends and family waved from their cars and pulled out of the driveway.

Brett helped Leila put a very sleepy Evie to bed. And finally, he was alone with her. It had grown cold as the day went on. Leila brewed a couple mugs of hot chocolate while he started a fire.

"I can't believe it's February already," she commented when she carried the mugs in and set them on the coffee table. "Before you know it, it will be time to turn on the air-conditioning again."

They settled on the couch in front of the fireplace. Brett took a sip from his mug. He played with Leila's hand, admiring the way her ring sparkled.

"Are you happy?" he murmured to Leila.

She nestled closer. "So happy. I know we only just got engaged today, and this is all new, but I can't wait to marry you and start our life together."

"I was thinking the same thing. How would you feel about an October wedding?"

She tilted her head and considered it. "That leaves us eight months. I think it sounds perfect."

"Almost as perfect as you, future Mrs. Talbot." Brett leaned over and sealed their agreement with a kiss. Her right hand brushed his cheek.

He could hardly contain the joy overwhelming his soul. He'd accepted that he'd be alone forever, but God had other plans.

Brett kissed his fiancée again, sending up a silent prayer of thanksgiving to their heavenly Father, who had brought light and love out of the darkness.

Brett held Leila in his arms and with his kiss promised to cherish her and love her for the rest of his life.

* * * * *

If you enjoyed this book, more titles by Dana R. Lynn are available now from Love Inspired!

Find more great reads at www.LoveInspired.com.

Dear Reader,

Thank you for reading Brett and Leila's story. This is the second book in the Amish Country Danger series. I love creating new characters and seeing what makes them tick.

I find myself very drawn to the theme of redemption and reconciliation. Both Brett and Leila have suffered severe traumas in their life. In the case of Leila, her past has caused her to reject God and abandon her faith. I enjoyed writing her return to God. Hers is very much the story of a prodigal child who rejected her earthly father and God and needed to find her way home.

I love hearing from readers! You can connect with me on social media or contact me at www.danarlynn.com. To hear information about upcoming books, sign up for my newsletter.

Blessings,
Dana R. Lynn